THE
DEVIL'S
GAME

ALEX STRONG

Cover Art © fotolia/ASjack/ninog
Cover design by J.P. Irons

ISBN: 978-0-9964709-6-4

What reviewers are saying…

"Alex Strong's writing flows so effortlessly, that it drew me in again and again…."

  -Steffi for TheRomanceReview.com

"I found it a delightful well written short read that once you start reading you it will keep your attention to the end. Would I recommend? Yes!"

  -Arlena for NightOwlReviews.com

"The author's writing is solid and robust. The plot and story line are good and different. The reader feels romance in the air."

"… the author has a knack for writing and keeping the interest of readers. The ability to control and keep the reader involved is strong."

  -Amazon Breakthrough Novel Award Expert Reviews

I dedicate this book to my husband. Simply because I love you.

The Encounter

KARINA HANDED THE cups to the barista behind her and faced the next customer. Her breath hitched slightly at the sight of him. His hazel eyes shining brightly against his caramel skin and jet-black hair were the most intense thing she'd ever seen, and though no interaction had occurred yet, she felt sure that she had done something wrong just by looking at him.

She cleared her throat. "What can I get you today, sir?"

"A grande macchiato, please," he said in the most exquisite voice ever—a warm baritone that gently caressed her ears. The fact that it came from such a sensual mouth only made it all the more seductive.

Karina tucked a loose strand of auburn hair behind her ear and forced herself to look at the cash register and ring up his coffee.

"That will be four dollars and eighty-five cents," she

told him, reaching for a sixteen-ounce cup and writing his order on it. "And can I get your name?"

"Excuse me?" he asked, and she risked looking at him. His eyebrow was raised, and again she felt as though she had slighted him.

"I need it for the order," she said quietly. "So it gets to the right person."

Just then, one of the baristas called out a customer's name.

He gave a slight nod. "Damien."

She wrote the name as he pulled cash from his wallet, and the transaction was completed. He stepped aside to wait for his drink as another customer walked up to the register. Karina was sure she could feel his gaze burning into her, but she didn't dare look his direction in case she was right.

Several more customers went through her line before she heard the name Damien called out, and this time, she couldn't help glancing his way, as though even his name held a power over her. She watched him grab his drink and quickly walk to the door, where he stopped and turned, giving her a quizzical look, then walked outside to where a man was waiting for him. When he was gone from sight, Karina released a ragged breath she didn't even realize she'd been holding.

"I'm sorry," she said to the customer who was telling her his order. "Could you repeat that one more time for me?"

As Karina finished the rest of her shift, she wondered if she would ever see Damien again. Part of her hoped she would, but there was also a small part that feared what would happen if she did.

Karina hit submit on the web page and glanced at the time in the corner of the screen.

"Shit," she muttered. It had taken too long to fill out that last form, and now she barely had time to make it to the coffee shop for her shift.

She logged off the library computer and grabbed the pile of papers and booklets next to it before rushing out the door. As she stepped out onto the sidewalk, Karina leafed through the pages in her arms, making sure she hadn't left anything behind, when she slammed right into another person and dropped everything.

She bent down to pick everything up. "I'm so sorry, I wasn't—" Karina looked up right into Damien's golden eyes.

He looked down at her questioningly. "You're the girl from the coffee shop." She nodded. "Karina." This time she frowned. "It was on your name tag," he explained.

Karina continued to gaze up at him, unsure what to do or say. He bent down and started helping her gather up the scattered papers.

"Are you a student?" he asked, pausing to look at a printout for a graduate program.

"Trying to be," she said, reaching for the paper. "I'm so sorry I ran into you like that. But I really need to get going or I'm going to be—"

Suddenly his hand closed around her wrist. "Have dinner with me," he said.

Her heart raced as she looked down at the long, tapered fingers touching her skin and was surprised she didn't feel the need to pull away.

"I—I can't," she said.

"Are you seeing someone?"

"What?" She frowned, looking up at him. "No, it's not that—"

"Do you know who I am?" he asked, looking slightly puzzled.

Karina studied him in his Burberry coat over the

tailored suit, a fancy watch on the wrist of the hand still gripping her. He was obviously well off, but there was nothing familiar about him.

"No," she said with a sidelong glance. "Should I?"

"I suppose not," he said, releasing her, and she slid the flyer from his fingers.

She stood, and he stood with her.

"Again, I'm sorry," she said and stepped around him, rushing off. She glanced over her shoulder to see him watching her, and she turned back around, walking even faster as her heart pounded in her chest.

Karina was in the back cleaning up when the front door chimed and she sighed. Michael had said they could leave a little early if no one else came in by the time she finished, but now he was going to insist they stay the last half hour.

She started to hang the broom back up but froze as soon as she heard the customer's voice.

"A grande macchiato," Damien said. "Decaf, please."

"Coming right up," said Michael.

Karina waited as Michael made the drink and then held her breath, listening for the chime signaling that Damien had left. He didn't need to know she was still there. But the sound never came. Instead, Michael walked into the back carrying one of the cash drawers.

"Do you mind watching the front while I count this till?"

Karina nodded and stepped hesitantly out into the seating area, where Damien was sitting at a table in the corner, not the least bit surprised to see her.

She should ignore him—start wiping the counters or something. But as he held her in his gaze, she let curiosity get the best of her and walked up to his table.

"Did you decide you needed one last coffee before heading home?" she asked, gripping the back of the empty chair across from him.

"Actually, I came to see if you would reconsider my invitation to dinner. But I couldn't very well just sit here waiting for you. Hence the coffee," he said, lifting his cup. She looked at the fingers wrapped around the cup and involuntarily grabbed her own wrist, remembering his touch.

"I'm afraid you've wasted your five dollars then," she said, putting her hand back on the chair. "Because the answer is still no."

Damien tilted his head. "Do you mind if I ask why?"

Who the hell *was* this guy? Had no one ever told him no before? Karina decided the truth might be her best defense. She turned to make sure Michael was still in the back before sitting in the empty seat.

"I can only think of two reasons you want me to go out with you," she told him. "You're looking for a one night stand, or you are seriously interested in dating me. Either way, I have too much on my plate for any distractions. In another life, I might have considered either offer," she said with a twinge of disappointment. "But unfortunately, your timing is off, so the answer's still no."

"I see," he said.

She watched and waited while he took a drink from his coffee.

"In that case," he continued, standing. "I should let you go for the night. I appreciate your being direct with me." And he left without saying anything else.

Karina sighed as she watched him walk away. Maybe someday, when things weren't such a mess, she could say yes for once.

There was a knock at Karina's bedroom door just before nine the next morning.

"What is it?" she asked, rolling over.

Her roommate Ginny popped her head in. "There's someone at the door for you. Were you expecting anyone?"

"No," Karina said, crinkling her nose. "Do you know who it is?"

Ginny shook her head. "He looks important though. And drop-dead gorgeous."

Damien was the first person to come to Karina's mind. But why would he be at her door? And how would he even know where she lives?

"Tell whoever it is I'll be right out," Karina said, grabbing the sweatshirt at the end of the bed to put over her tank top and throwing back the covers. The thin leggings did little to stop the chill as she climbed out of the warm bed. She walked into the living room to find Damien standing by the door, looking completely out of place in the tiny apartment.

"Good morning," he said, his eyes brightening at the sight of her.

"Morning," she replied with a frown. This was getting creepy.

"I'll just grab my coffee and then go get ready for work," said Ginny. She gave Karina a look as she walked back to her bedroom, and Karina knew she wanted details later.

"How did you find me?" Karina demanded as soon as Ginny's door clicked shut.

"It was easy enough," he said, not really answering her question.

"But you don't know my last name," she said. "My name isn't even on the lease."

"Do you mind if we sit?" he asked. "I have a proposition I would like to make."

Karina knew that she should send this man away. Call the cops if he refused to leave. But her curiosity about him got the best of her yet again, and she moved to the middle of the couch while he took a seat in the chair angled toward her. Damien didn't look uncomfortable in it, but the whole space felt too small for him, too dull. Or maybe that was just her.

"So what's your proposition?" she asked, crossing her arms.

"I've looked into your situation—"

"Who the hell do you think you are?"

"—and I want to offer my help," he finished.

"And what exactly is it that you think you know about my situation?"

"I know that your mother was recently sick and lost her job because of it."

Karina shook her head.

"And now your parents are buried in medical debt and about to lose their house."

"That is none of your business."

"This is why you are applying for every scholarship available for graduate school."

"Why do you even care?" she asked.

"When there is something that I want, I have a talent for exploiting opportunities to get it."

"And what exactly is it that you want?" she asked, though she suspected she knew the answer.

"Simple. I want you."

Karina's breath hitched at his words. "And you're willing to help my parents out just so I will go on a date with you?"

The corner of his seductive mouth went up ever so slightly. "It would entail a bit more than that."

"Of course it would," she said, narrowing her eyes at him.

"I am willing to pay off all of your parents' debt," Karina's jaw dropped, "if you agree to come live with me for a month."

"You do realize we're talking hundreds of thousands?" Damien didn't flinch.

"At the conclusion of the month," he continued, "I will provide you with enough money to finish your schooling."

This was wrong; Karina knew this was so wrong. She needed to end this conversation right now.

"Why?" she asked instead.

"This is a one-time offer," he said, again avoiding her question. "I need an answer from you."

She should say no. This was ridiculous. This man was *crazy*. But, oh god, what if he was serious? This could change everything for her and her parents. It was only a month. Surely she could handle being someone's plaything for thirty days if it solved all her problems. Even entertaining the thought made her sick to her stomach, though. She looked at Damien, who sat there patiently waiting for her response.

This was a joke. It had to be. Someone—whether it was Damien or some other sick bastard—was messing with her. Although she couldn't imagine why.

"Fine," she said as she stood, deciding to call his bluff. "You do everything you just promised, and in return, I will come live with you."

She walked to the door and held it open for him.

"So we have a deal then?" he asked, standing.

"Sure. As soon as I get confirmation that everything has been settled"—Karina knew this would take months—"I will be all yours for a whole month."

"I'll be in touch," he said, walking out into the hall.

"Looking forward to it," she said sarcastically.

"You should probably give notice at work," he said before she could close the door.

"You're saying I won't be allowed to work while I'm with you?"

"Well, I live in Miami. I'm only here on business."

"Miami?"

"Ah, yes, I keep forgetting you don't know who I am," he said, extending a hand that she refused to take. "Damien Bishop." He withdrew the hand. "Take care, Karina," he said with a nod, then walked away.

She closed the door and dead bolted it. Why, she wasn't sure, but it made her feel better. Karina needed to look up Damien and figure out who this lunatic was.

"Ginny," she called out, rushing to the bedroom door, which immediately swung open. "Can I borrow your laptop?" Karina asked.

"Who was that?" Ginny asked, letting Karina into the room.

"I'm not sure," Karina said as she sat at Ginny's desk and typed Damien's name into the search box. "That's what I want to look up. He said his name was Damien Bishop."

"Damien Bishop? You don't mean *the* Damien Bishop, do you?"

Karina swung around in the chair to face Ginny, who was dressed for work, a brush mid-stroke through her long blonde hair.

"I don't know. Who is Damien Bishop?"

"He's the billionaire tech guru," Ginny said, and Karina's stomach did a somersault.

"Where is he based out of?" Karina asked nervously.

"He has businesses all over the world, but I think his headquarters are in Florida. Miami maybe."

Karina closed her eyes, but then opened them again.

"What's he doing up here then?"

"He's in town for the big expo. Start-ups compete, hoping he'll invest. It's a big deal because every company he chooses has gone on to be huge. My bank is one of the event sponsors." Ginny laid the brush on the dresser and picked up her purse. "So was that *the* Damien?"

"It couldn't be," Karina said as she turned back to the computer. One look at the image that had popped up and she knew she was wrong.

"I have to go or I'll be late," said Ginny. "But when I get home tonight, you're going to tell me why he was in our living room."

"I close again tonight," Karina muttered.

"Fine, when *you* get home. I'll have the wine open. Maybe I'll even save you a glass," she said with a giggle as she left the room. Karina heard Ginny struggle with the front door, which was still dead bolted. And then she was gone, and Karina sat there, staring at Damien's picture, cursing the day he had walked into her coffee shop because she was sure there was no way this was going to end well.

Karina got so caught up in researching Damien that she barely made it to work on time again. As she tried to focus, all the facts kept swirling in her head. He was born in Puerto Rico but had spent most of his upbringing in Miami, Florida, which was probably why he kept his primary residence and main offices there. The guy apparently had several of them, including a vacation home in France. When he was nineteen, attending MIT, both parents were killed in a car crash, leaving him a considerable inheritance that he has since vastly improved. He recently celebrated his thirty-first birthday, which made him almost seven years older than her, but had never been married. And judging by all the pictures Karina had clicked through, Damien didn't have long-term girlfriends. He was never photographed with the same woman twice, and even those photos looked chaste. Nothing to suggest anything intimate going on.

But the scariest information of all—at least as far as Karina was concerned—was the fact that he was worth 1.2 billion dollars. Which meant that a couple hundred thousand was chump change to him.

By the time Karina got home that night, her stomach was in knots, and she was grateful to find that Ginny had received a more enticing offer at a nearby bar. She immediately crawled into bed, where she mostly tossed and turned long after Ginny stumbled home. Would Damien really go through with it? And if he did, would she be able to keep up her end of the bargain?

She cursed her alarm when it went off at five the next morning, but at least she would be able to sneak out for work before Ginny woke. She had no idea what to say to her and dreaded what Ginny might think of her for agreeing—even if it was only because Karina never imagined he could've been serious.

As Karina mulled it over at work that day, she realized the solution was simple. When she got home, she would figure out some way to get a hold of Damien and let him know that she had changed her mind. Yes, her parents would lose their house (a heartbreaking thought), but Karina knew they would never want her to sell her self-respect for it. They would've been appalled that she had even considered it.

When she got off work, she pulled her phone from her bag to see that she had missed a call from her mom. She listened to the voicemail asking her to call back as she walked out of the shop and toward home.

"Hey Mom, what's up?" Karina asked as soon as her mom answered.

"The strangest thing happened! Well, I just don't know what to make of it. I mean, I know your father and I have been praying about it every night, but I never imagined…."

"Mom," Karina said. "Slow down. What have you been praying about?"

"A courier just stopped by an hour ago, which was so odd. I mean, I didn't know those still existed, I just thought everybody used FedEx or whatever."

Karina sighed. It always took her mother forever to explain anything. "What did the courier drop off?"

"Papers saying that the house has been paid off." Karina stopped dead in her tracks. "I'm holding the deed to the house in my hands right now. Or at least a copy of it. Apparently it's been filed somewhere for safekeeping."

"Oh god," Karina whispered.

"I know, right!" her mother exclaimed. "And that's not all. There's even statements in here showing that all the hospital bills have been paid in full."

Karina stumbled over to some nearby steps and fell down onto them.

"You know what this mean, sweetie, don't you?" her mom asked.

"Yes," Karina managed to say.

"It means we aren't losing the house! You could move back home if you wanted to. You could finally afford to go back to school."

Her mother was so happy, so *relieved*, and Karina didn't want to be the one to take that away from her, no matter the cost.

"That's great news, Mom. I'll, uh, I'll have to get back to you about moving back in or not."

"Okay sweetie. Your dad wants to go celebrate. Talk to you soon. Oh, honey, our prayers have been answered!"

"Yes, Mom, they have."

Karina hung up the phone knowing that those prayers had been answered because she'd made a deal with the devil.

The Devil Collects

KARINA SLOWLY MADE her way back home, wondering how long it would be before she heard from Damien. (Probably not long, judging by how quickly he took care of the house and bills.) She walked in to find Ginny sprawled out on the couch, a water bottle and bag of chips nearby. Karina saw this as a good sign, as Ginny was never very talkative when she was hungover.

"Someone dropped a package off for you," Ginny said without even looking up from the TV. "It's over on the counter."

The manila envelope stood out ominously against the blue linoleum. Karina imagined it looked just like the one that had been delivered to her parents today. She tore it open and slid out copies of the same documents her mother had received, but this pack had a handwritten note paper-clipped to it.

Karina,

As per your request, here is confirmation that your parents' debt has been taken care of. I am sending a car at 11 a.m. tomorrow to pick you up; please be ready by then. Only pack the most important items you need for the month, as everything else will be provided for you. I've enclosed a check to cover your portion of the following month's rent.

Damien

The note was cold and professional, and it made her stomach tighten that much more. Tomorrow morning. Less than twenty-four hours until she ran off with this man, this stranger.

She looked at the check made out to Ginny. Virginia A. Redding, to be exact. Karina pulled it from the stack and walked over to the chair Damien had sat in only yesterday.

"This is for you," she said, handing the check to Ginny.

"What's this for?" she asked.

"It's my rent for next month."

"But why—" Ginny's eyes went wide. "Holy shit, this check is from Damien Bishop! Why is Damien Bishop giving me a check for your rent?"

Karina took a deep breath. "Because I'm going to be with him for the next month."

Ginny's eyes went even wider, and then she smiled, and Karina felt sick.

"Are you sleeping with him?"

Karina shook her head, and Ginny's forehead wrinkled.

"Then why are you going away with him?"

Karina finally spilled the whole story. When she finished, Ginny looked to be in awe where Karina had expected disgust.

"Wow," said Ginny. "I'm so jealous."

"Jealous? Are you kidding me?"

"He just solved all your problems and now you get to spend the next month by his hot, gorgeous side. Of course I'm jealous."

"But I don't know the man!"

"You know that he's rich," Ginny said. "And built like a Greek god."

"Do you realize he could be some psychopath? In fact, I'm starting to think that he is. This is not what normal people do!"

Ginny shook her head. "I'd bear it for thirty days."

"Then maybe you should trade places with me."

"Gladly."

Karina remembered Damien's words to her yesterday morning. *I want you.* She doubted he would accept a substitute. Even a more attractive one, in her opinion.

"I should go pack," she said, knowing that Ginny would never see it from her side. "Not to mention call the shop and my parents to let them know I won't be around for a month."

"Try not to sound so excited about it," Ginny called out as Karina walked out of the room.

"Fuck you," Karina called over her shoulder and shut the door.

By that night, Karina had packed all the items she deemed necessary to get through the next month and had made the dreaded phone calls. She told the shop that there had been a family emergency and that she would be out of town for a month. Her boss had been annoyed about the short notice, but even he agreed it would be easy to fill her shifts. Everyone was looking for more hours these days.

Lying to her parents had been harder. If they wouldn't have thought it odd not to see her for a whole month, she might not have said anything and just claimed to be busy whenever they tried to plan anything. In the end, she told them that the coffee shop was opening a new store in Miami and they had asked her to go down and help get it going. She figured that way they would know where to go looking for the body if she never came home. Not that Karina really expected it to come to that. Damien had left his fingerprints everywhere.

Her dad seemed a little suspicious, but Karina's mom was excited for her—she thought it was an honor for Karina to be asked and the perfect opportunity to escape the dreary spring they were having.

Karina was exhausted when she climbed into bed that night, but sleep eluded her just as much as the night before. She tried not to, but she kept glancing at the clock, counting down. Ten hours until Damien came for her. Nine…eight…seven….

Karina woke early the next morning despite the few hours she had managed to sleep, and she showered and dressed before moving her bags out to the living room, leaving them ready by the door. She made a cup of coffee and then sat by the window, staring out at the gray drizzle covering the streets. As she pulled the blanket from the couch to wrap around her shoulders, Karina wondered what the weather was like in Miami right now. Was it really as hot as they showed in the movies? It occurred to her that this would be the first time Karina had ventured beyond the neighboring states. If only she could get excited about the idea.

At half past ten, Ginny wandered out of her bedroom. She poured the last of the coffee into a mug and came to stand by Karina.

"Did you tell your parents?" she asked before taking a sip.

Karina shook her head. "They know I'm going to be in Miami, but they couldn't bear this."

"I'm sorry I acted so heartless yesterday," Ginny said, putting an arm around Karina.

"It's okay," Karina. "I realize it probably sounds like a fairy tale, it's just that—"

"I know."

They stood for a while in silence, enjoying the warmth of the coffee.

"Call me every day," Ginny finally said. "Let me know that you're okay."

Karina nodded, fighting back tears. What had she done?

A black sedan came gliding down the street and double parked right in front of their building.

"Is that him?" Ginny asked.

"It must be," Karina choked out.

They watched a man in slacks and a sweater climb out of the driver's side and head for the front entrance.

"Good luck," Ginny said, giving Karina one last hug.

"Thanks." Karina slung her purse across her chest and opened the door just as the driver came up the steps.

"Karina Watson?" he asked.

She nodded and started to roll out the suitcase, but he stopped her.

"I've got it," he said. "I can take care of that as well." He pointed to the small duffle bag on the floor next to it.

Karina stepped aside and let him pick it up.

"Is there anything else?" he asked, and she shook her head.

He headed back down the stairs. She turned to Ginny, not really sure what to say.

"I guess I'll talk to you later," Karina told her and followed after the driver, leaving Ginny to close the door behind her. It wasn't until she was halfway down the steps that she finally heard it shut, and Karina swallowed hard.

Outside, the driver set the bags down before opening the passenger door for her. She held her breath as she looked into the car and was shocked to find it empty.

"Where's Damien?" she asked.

"Mr. Bishop will be meeting us at the plane, Ma'am."

Karina looked up at the window where she knew Ginny would be watching, gave a wave, and then climbed into the back seat.

Not a word was spoken the entire trip; the driver didn't even attempt to make small talk. Karina stared out the tinted windows the whole time and was surprised when they pulled into a small, private airfield.

Of course, Damien Bishop had his own jet. The thought made Karina even more nervous. She had imagined them flying down to Miami with a hundred other passengers and some flight attendants who would distract her from what she was really doing on that plane. Instead, she was going to be stuck in a confined space with only her and Damien. She wondered if he would expect anything from her so soon.

The car stopped near the door to the plane. The driver was quick to let her out, then immediately started unloading her bags along with others that must have already been packed before she'd been picked up. He didn't give any direction, and Karina assumed she was supposed to board the plane.

Slowly, cautiously, she climbed each step and discovered she was wrong about her and Damien being the only ones on the plane.

A man close to her age, maybe a year or two older, greeted her the second she set foot in the cabin, and another one—definitely older and more somber-looking—was seated nearby.

"You must be Karina Watson," the younger one said with a cheerful smile.

Karina gave a single, slow nod.

"My name is Tom. Damien had hoped to be here to

greet you personally, but it seems he's been delayed slightly. He should be here any minute though," he said hurriedly, as though reassuring her. "He's asked that I help you get settled and make sure you're comfortable. May I show you to your seat?"

"Um, okay."

The interior of the plane was the most luxurious thing Karina had ever seen. Warm beiges and sleek wood paneling made it feel inviting to her. There was only a single row of seats along each side of the plane, but each one was roomy and plush with padded armrests and high backs. As she sat in the one she was led to, Karina suspected it even reclined.

"Can I get you anything?" Tom asked as she sat down. "Coffee? Sparkling water? Champagne, perhaps?"

"Just water is fine," she said. "Plain water. Not sparkling."

"Very well, then," he said and disappeared into the back of the plane only to quickly reappear with a glass of ice and a bottle of water.

Tom placed them both on a flat, recessed area of the paneling beneath the window.

"Will that be all?" he asked, and Karina nodded. "Damien should be back any minute," he repeated just as something out the window seemed to catch his eye. "Oh look, there he is now."

Tom rushed to wait by the door, and Karina looked out the window to see a black limousine parked outside. A man climbed out of the passenger side front and opened the rear door. Karina inhaled sharply as Damien emerged. He was laughing and appeared to be talking to someone still in the limo. He nodded to whoever it was and walked away, letting the other man close the door before following Damien to the plane.

Tom greeted Damien just as exuberantly, but Karina

could only stare at the empty seat facing her, her heart pounding wildly in her chest.

"Is everything ready?" she heard him ask Tom.

"Yes, sir," Tom replied. "Jim is just waiting for your word, and Miss Watson has arrived and is seated."

"Good. Tell him to take off. And bring me a glass of scotch as soon as we're in the air."

"Of course."

Karina heard the soft footsteps coming her way and thought for sure that her heart would burst, it was beating so furiously.

Damien sat down opposite her, facing her, and Karina couldn't *not* look him in the eye. It was the same intense look he had given her at the coffee shop. Good god, was that really only three days ago?

"Karina," Damien said in that sensuous voice of his.

It was hunger, she realized. The look in his eyes was hunger. For her. And Karina feared she wouldn't survive it.

"Damien," she said, fighting to keep her voice even.

The plane started to roll forward, and Karina found herself gripping the arm rests.

"Everything okay?" he asked, tilting his head.

"It's fine," she said a bit harshly.

"Have you ever flown before?"

"Don't you already know the answer to that?" she asked, and he frowned. "You seem to know everything else about me."

He sighed. "I only gathered the info that I needed to help you."

"That's what this is? Helping me?"

"You're here, aren't you? Of your own accord, I might add."

The engines started to roar, and Karina felt herself sink deeper into the chair as the plane accelerated. She closed her eyes, waiting for it to be over with, and felt something on her knee.

She opened her eyes to see Damien leaning forward with his hand on her.

"There's nothing to be afraid of," Damien told her.

Karina wondered if he meant the plane ride or him.

"How long until we land?" she asked.

He leaned back in his seat. "It's about a three-hour flight depending on the wind."

Karina dared a look back at the other three passengers. "So who are they?" she asked.

"Tom is my personal assistant. The other two men are part of my security team. You'll undoubtedly see a lot of them, but they don't talk much."

"Do you always travel with bodyguards?"

"I do."

"I see," she said when he didn't elaborate. "How did the expo go?" Karina finally asked, not sure what else to talk about.

"Not as well as I'd hoped, but I found a couple of promising candidates I'd like to look into more."

Just then, Tom appeared.

"Thank you," Damien said as Tom handed him a glass of something gold.

"Are you two hungry?" Tom asked. "Should I bring out lunch?"

Damien looked at her. "Are you ready to eat?"

The mention of food reminded Karina how long it had been since her last meal, and she nodded.

"Then yes please," Damien said. "And bring a bottle of Viognier with it."

Karina waited for Tom to disappear before she leaned forward and asked, "What is vee-oh-nee-a?"

Damien leaned forward until he was only inches from her face, and she could smell his subtle yet intoxicating aftershave. "It's a white wine," he whispered.

She sat back in her chair feeling embarrassed.

"Are you a wine drinker?" he asked. "I could request something else."

"No, it's fine," she said. "Yes, I drink wine. It's just— it's just that my exposure is generally limited to whatever my roommate brings home."

"I see," he said. "Well, perhaps we can remedy that during your time with me."

Karina looked at him, so many questions running through her head. What exactly were his expectations of her during that time? She was afraid to know the answer.

A phone started ringing, and Damien fished it out of his suit pocket. He frowned as he looked at it.

"I apologize," he said, standing, "but I have to take this." He moved to a seat at the back of the cabin, taking his scotch with him, and Karina turned her attention to the clouds outside her window. When did they get this high? She had been so distracted with Damien she hadn't noticed anything beyond the take-off.

Tom arrived to pull a tabletop from the panel beneath the window and brought a tray of salads and the wine shortly after. Karina glanced back at Damien as Tom filled her glass.

"It might be a while," Tom said with a small frown. "I wouldn't wait. Just in case."

"Thank you," she said and Tom left.

Karina waited a couple minutes and then started on her spicy Thai salad. She was just about to take the last bite when Tom delivered a thin slice of cheesecake topped with dark cherries. She wondered if he was always this efficient.

The plates were cleared, including Damien's, and Tom refilled her glass and set it on the side before putting the table away, but Damien was still on the phone. Karina found the button to pull the footrest out and enjoyed the wine in silence. With a little bit of alcohol and some food in her, the last few nights were finally catching up to her. She didn't know she had fallen asleep until a harsh jolt woke her up. Damien was sitting across from her again, and she was wrapped up in a blanket.

"We're here," he said.

The First Night

KARINA LOOKED OUT the window to see them speeding along the runway, but the plane was slowing quickly. Just the bright sunshine would have been enough to let Karina know she wasn't home anymore, but the palm trees and vividly colored buildings felt like an entirely different world.

The plane came to a complete stop at the end of the runway, where a black SUV was parked, and Damien stood and waited for Karina. She pushed the blanket to one side and followed him to the exit. The door opened, and Karina was hit by a blast of warm, humid air.

"*Bienvenido a Miami,*" Damien said from her side.

The Spanish from his lips only made his voice that much more seductive, and she resisted the urge to look at his mouth.

As they climbed down the steps, Karina couldn't but help feel a twinge of excitement.

"Let's get in the car before we melt," Damien said, and he let Tom and one of the bodyguards climb in the back before having Karina crawl into the middle row, where he slid in next to her.

The air conditioned interior felt much better for Karina, who had chosen a sweater and jeans that rainy morning back at home. She knew Damien must have felt the same in his dark suit.

Again the car ride was quiet—except this time for the sound of Damien typing on his phone—but Karina was content to watch the landscape go by. Even the people were so different. They had plenty of variety back home, but everyone there seemed to dress the same. It was easy, especially this time of year, to get lost in a sea of bland jackets and knitted scarves and hats. Not here, though. Karina couldn't remember ever seeing so many different colors on so many bodies. And there was so much skin, especially as they drove along the beaches. The two-pieces she'd packed were starting to feel prudish compared to what many of the women were wearing. Even some of the men weren't leaving much to the imagination.

The landscape soon changed to quieter, more subdued tree-lined streets. The ocean became obscured by large homes barely visible behind overbearing gates and walls. The driveways were so intermittent that at first she thought they led to apartment complexes. It finally occurred to her that it was testament to the size of the private properties.

And then they were pulling into one those driveways. A gate opened, allowing them access. The car continued up a long driveway, and Karina gasped as the most breath-taking house came into view.

"Do you like it?" Damien asked. She had almost forgotten he was in the car with her.

"It's beautiful," she whispered. It was simple in its design—white stucco with straight lines and metallic elements. But the rest of the property seemed to curve around it, from the steps leading up to the front door to the shrubbery and walkways, creating sleek, sensual lines around the expansive two-story structure.

The car stopped, and the bodyguard who had been riding in the front seat opened the door on Damien's side. He climbed out and then offered a hand to help Karina, who had almost forgotten her nervousness. If only Ginny could see her now.

They walked into a grand foyer with its vaulted ceilings and a sweeping staircase leading up to the second floor. To her right was a formal sitting room complete with a grand piano.

"Let me give you the tour," Damien said, and he led her through the house.

It was hard to remember why she was here as he showed her the elegant dining room, the gourmet kitchen, and even an entertainment room. At the back of the house was a sunroom, and next to that was a personal gym with sliding walls that opened to the outside. Behind the house was a full-sized swimming pool, a guest house, and beyond that, the ocean. A small canal cut into the property, a sailing boat docked on the pier.

They moved upstairs, and Karina's nervousness started to return as he showed her the bedrooms.

"And this room is yours," he said, opening a door.

"Mine?" she asked, confused.

"Yes. My bedroom is right next door." He looked at his watch. "Dinner will be served in the dining room at seven. I'll leave you to get settled and freshen up."

He strode off down the hall to his room and Karina stepped into her own, closing the door behind her as she took in the space. It was almost as big as the apartment she shared with Ginny and was decorated in powder blue and white trim with pewter accents. There was a pair of French doors leading to a balcony overlooking the pool, a door for the closet, and one that opened to her very own bathroom. Now *that* she was looking forward to.

Her bags were already at the foot of the king-sized bed, waiting to be unpacked, and she walked over to them and sank onto the silver satin comforter. She had tried not to think about where she would be sleeping, but Karina never imagined she would have her own bedroom. Perhaps sleeping was all she was meant to do in this room. Was it to be that kind of arrangement? On the plus side, she wasn't tied up in a dungeon yet. Speaking of which, Karina decided she should check in with Ginny to let her know so far, so good.

The call went to voicemail, and Karina left a message letting her know she had arrived safely. The time shown there was a little less than an hour until dinner, so she started to unpack. She rolled the suitcase to the closet and found it to be almost as big as her bedroom back home and already filled with amazing clothes. Wondering who they could belong to, she perused the labels. Many designers she recognized, quite a few she didn't. It didn't take long for Karina to realize that every single one was in her size. Were these meant for her? And how did he know her size? She found a shelf of shoes and tried one on. It was a beautiful nude pump with a red sole. She didn't have to read the name on it to know it was a Christian Louboutin. Or that the pair of them were probably worth more than all the shoes she had in her closet back home. Again, the perfect size. But *how*?

A knock at the bedroom door made her jump, and she dropped the shoe, slipping her flat back on. She opened the door to find Tom on the other side, holding a garment bag and a laptop.

"This just arrived," he said, handing her the Mac notebook. "Sorry it wasn't here sooner."

"Um, thank you?" Karina said, not really sure what she was supposed to say.

"And Damien has suggested that you wear this for dinner tonight."

"Oh," Karina said, taking the bag from him. "Okay."

"Is the room to your liking?" he asked. "Do you need anything else?"

"No, it's perfect. Thank you." She started to close the door. "Wait," she said, opening it again. She looked around to make sure Damien wasn't within ear-shot. "Whose clothes are those in the closet?"

Tom frowned. "They're yours, of course. I tried to get a selection of current items, though a couple were directly requested by Damien. Are they not what you were expecting?"

"No, it's just that…how did you know what size to buy?"

"Damien told me, of course." As if that explained everything.

"Well, thank you," she told him again.

He gave a nod and walked away. She shut the door and laid the laptop on a bedside table before moving back to the closet with the garment bag. There was a hook just inside the door that she hung the bag on and unzipped it. Inside was a simple navy silk dress. She tore off her clothes and tried it on. The thin material caressed her skin as it slipped on with ease. With a turn of her stomach, Karina realized it probably slipped off just as easily. She bent over and braced her hands on her knees, taking several deep breaths. She could do this. It was just like any other date she had been on. He wouldn't be the first man she had slept with— far from it. He would, however, be the first to have bribed her for sex, though. A couple more deep breaths. Hopefully alcohol was served with dinner, because she was going to need all the liquid courage she could get.

Karina walked into the dining room promptly at seven, a familiar pounding in her chest, to find Damien standing at the head of the table waiting for her. It was the first time she had seen him without his suit on, but he looked just as polished in slate-colored slacks and a crisp white shirt that looked that much brighter against his dark complexion.

"You look amazing," he whispered as she approached, and Karina caught the same hungry look in his eyes.

"I suppose I have you to thank for that," she said tartly. "You did request the dress, after all."

"I figured you might not know what to wear for the first night," he said, holding out a chair for her. "I wanted to make it easier for you."

"Do you always get dressed up for dinner in your own home?" she asked as she sat down and let him push the chair in.

"Only when I have guests," he said, sitting in his own chair.

"Do you have guests often?" Karina immediately reached for the glass already filled with red wine and took a large gulp.

"From time to time. Truth is, I'm not home that often. How do you like the wine?" he asked.

"It's really good, actually," she answered honestly and took another, slightly smaller drink.

"It's a Bordeaux blend," he said, swirling his glass. "One of my favorites."

"Good choice." Another sip.

"Do you like the room?" he asked as he dug into the salad before him. "If there's anything you'd like changed—"

"It's fine," she said, taking a small bite. The appetite she'd had on the plane had disappeared again. "How did you know my size?" she asked suddenly.

"I'm good at sizing people up," he said, refilling her already almost empty glass.

"But my shoe size—how could you possibly guess that?"

"I saw your feet when I came to your apartment. Though I admit I wasn't sure I had that one right. Have you tried any of them on?"

"I'm wearing a pair now," she said. "They're a perfect fit."

"Good."

Karina drank from her glass again, finally feeling the warmth start to spread through her.

"Are you not hungry?" Damien asked.

"I have a confession to make."

"Yes?"

"I find this all unnerving," she said.

"I don't blame you."

"Do you do this often?" she asked, feeling more brazen.

"You're the first," he said quietly.

She was about to ask why her, but a woman walked into the dining room carrying a tray. She took the salad plates and replaced them with dinner plates of salmon and colorful veggies. Karina went to take another drink only to find that her glass was mysteriously empty already. She waited a moment to see if Damien would refill it again, finally deciding to refill it herself when he didn't.

"You should really try this salmon," he said, gesturing to her untouched dinner. "It's Alaskan salmon. So much more flavor than the stuff from our ocean."

Karina forced a bite down. It did taste better than any fish she'd ever had, but she just couldn't stomach it right now, so she reached for the wine glass again only to have Damien stop her by placing his hand over the top of it.

"You might want to slow down," he said.

"I'm fine," she said, pulling the glass out from under

his hand. Wine sloshed against the side but managed to stay in its container. He frowned but said nothing.

Soon the dinner plates were taken away and a ramekin of dessert was placed before her.

"It's lava cake," he said.

She took a bite before pouring the last of the wine bottle into her glass.

"Do you normally drink like this?" Damien asked in what sounded like a scolding tone.

"You mean you don't already know?" Karina was aware that her words were slightly slurred.

"I told you—"

"Yes, yes, I know. Only enough info to 'help' me." She punctuated it by chugging the rest of the glass, and as she set down the glass, she knew she had overdone it.

"Will you excuse me?" she asked as she stood and nearly fell over.

Damien was on his feet in an instant, trying to help her.

"I've got this," she said. "Just give me a minute. Please."

Damien let go of her and Karina made her way to the stairs, focusing all her energy on staying upright. The journey to her room took entirely too long, and she barely made it to the toilet in time. It was nothing but red, and she vaguely wondered if she would notice if her insides came up with it, because by the time she was done, she felt hollow. She stood over the toilet a few more minutes, gripping the ceramic bowl, before remembering that Damien was still downstairs waiting for her. She just needed to clean up a bit first.

The shower stall was right next to her, and Karina reached in shakily to turn the water on. Once it was warmed up, she stepped in. It wasn't until she was in a ball on the floor that she realized she was still fully clothed. What had possessed her to drink that much wine, and so quickly? Now she just wanted to sleep, but when she closed her eyes the room started to spin. She tried to ignore it but just ended up vomiting right there in the shower. It was official—the dress was ruined.

There was a tapping on the door, but Karina was sure she was imagining it.

"Karina?"

"Go away," she called out. Or at least she thought she did. Her voice sounded so far away.

"You need to get of here before you drown."

"I'm fine," she mumbled. "I just need a few minutes." She thought she might be crying, but it was hard to tell in the shower.

The water stopped falling on her and the dress was pulled—ripped, maybe—off of her. Here it comes, she thought. Time to pay up. But then something warm and plush was wrapped around her and she felt herself being lifted off the floor and soon after, lowered onto a cloud. A warm, fluffy cloud. What felt like a gentle hand brushed her face, pushing the wet hair from her cheek as her mind went utterly and blissfully black.

Expectations

KARINA WANTED NOTHING more than to continue sleeping when she returned to consciousness the next morning, but her aching head wouldn't allow it any longer. She opened her eyes, trying to focus on the popcorn ceiling above her bed, except that it wasn't popcorn. It was smooth, and pure white rather than graying. She sat up, her brain screaming, and looked around. Damien's house. It all came back to her. Including the disaster that was last night. In a panic, she looked down to find that while the dress was gone, her underwear were still intact and she was wrapped in a robe. Nothing had happened last night, thanks to her. Karina wondered how mad Damien would be. And then she noticed the water glass and a bottle of ibuprofen on the table next to her. She opened the bottle and let two pills drop into her palm. She studied them, hesitant. But they didn't look suspicious, and she desperately wanted the pounding in her head to go away, so she swallowed them, washing them down with half the water.

She continued to lie in bed, waiting for relief, when she heard a splash outside the balcony doors. Cautiously, she climbed out and tied the robe around her. She opened a door and stepped out onto the balcony to see Damien swimming the length of the pool. When he got to one end, he tucked under and disappeared for a split second before reappearing, swimming just as strong in the opposite direction. Karina couldn't help but watch the impressive machine. A phone started ringing, bringing her out of her reverie, and she realized it was coming from the poolside. Damien heard it as well and swam toward it.

"Hello," she heard him say with his back to her. He was standing in the shallower end, and she could see the muscles in his back ripple with every movement.

"That's not what I asked," he said. "You need to figure this out. If I do your job for you, then I have no need for you." He paused, running a hand through his dark, wet hair. "I see. Then how about if I go take a look right now, and if I manage to find a solution before you…. Good man. Call me when it's done."

Damien hung up the phone and then pulled himself out of the pool to sit on the ledge. He was now facing her direction. Karina took a step back, but it only seemed to attract his attention and he looked up at her, his expression unreadable. This time, she was sure she had done something wrong, and she went back into her room. She climbed back into bed and pulled her knees up to her chin, wrapping her arms around her legs, and waited. Waited for Damien to come and punish her, or have his way with her, or something. She looked at the clock and realized it had been over twenty-four hours and the man had yet to even kiss her.

But Damien never came. She thought she heard him walk by a couple times, sometimes pausing briefly at her door, but he never knocked, and she couldn't even be sure it was him. And now she was getting hungry. Everything still ached and she dreaded going downstairs, but she couldn't stay up here and starve. She needed a shower first—a proper one—so she went into the bathroom and found last night's dress in the garbage. She could only imagine how much it had cost, and she had completely trashed it. Keep this up and Damien may just cut his losses and send her home.

When she walked back out into the bedroom wrapped in a towel and feeling more human, she found a tray of food on the table where the water and painkillers had been earlier. The glass, empty when she'd taken her shower, was now full again, and there was an assortment of warm pastries and fresh chilled fruit. It was delicious, and before she knew it, everything was gone. If food had been brought to her, then perhaps she wasn't expected to leave her room today. A panic swept through her, and she rushed to the door and tried to open it. She breathed a sigh of relief when the handle turned. She wasn't a prisoner after all. But then what was she?

Nightfall came, and Karina was still hiding out in her room. She felt the familiar butterflies, wondering if Damien would come for her tonight. She'd spent the whole afternoon reading but set her e-book aside, no longer able to concentrate. She turned off the lights and pulled the covers to her chin. Maybe if she pretended to be asleep when he came in, he would let her be. At around ten o'clock, she heard footsteps coming down the hall. Karina held her breath, but they continued right past her door to Damien's room, and a strange thought crept into her mind. Did Damien regret bringing her here? Did he no longer want her? Not that it would bother her, she told herself as she drifted off to sleep.

The next morning, Karina woke feeling restless. There was no way she was going to spend another day in the room. And it occurred to her that she may owe Damien an apology, because the truth was that he had been nothing but gracious so far. Which only made the whole thing more confusing. Maybe it had never been about sex.

I want you. His words echoed in her head. What did he want her for?

She dressed in her old, comfortable jeans but slipped on a sleeveless top from her recently acquired wardrobe. The ride to the house alone had shown Karina that the majority of what she'd brought was not exactly Miami attire.

The house was eerily still when she came down the stairs, and Karina wondered if she was the only one in it.

"Hello?" Her voice echoed into emptiness. But then she heard a noise from the kitchen. She headed in that direction and found the same woman who had delivered dinner the first night.

"Good morning," she said to Karina.

"Um, hi. Is Damien around?"

"I'm afraid he had to fly out to LA on urgent business. He says he will try to be back by tomorrow night. You're to make yourself at home."

"Oh." What was Karina supposed to do with herself for two days? "I'm sorry, I never caught your name the other night."

"It's Romi," she said with a pleasant smile

"Were you the one who brought the food to my room yesterday?" Karina asked.

"Oh, no," she said. "That was Mr. Bishop. We were asked not to disturb you yesterday."

"Who's we?"

Romi shrugged. "Staff in general. Security, me, whoever was around."

"Huh," said Karina. "This is going to sound weird, but am I allowed to leave the house?"

Romi gave her a strange expression. "I don't see why not."

"So it's fine if I decide to go for a walk around the neighborhood?"

Romi's brow furrowed even more.

Aha! Karina knew it.

"You could, but I wouldn't recommend it," Romi told her.

"Why not?"

"Not many people walk around the neighborhood. You'd probably end up getting stopped by security wondering who you are. And with Mr. Bishop away, we might have a harder time proving it's okay for you to be here."

Karina sighed.

"But a car can be arranged for you if you'd like to go somewhere else. Mr. Bishop said to make sure everything is at your disposal," Romi explained as she walked over to a drawer and pulled out an envelope. "And he wanted me to give you this."

She handed it to Karina, who peeked inside and saw several dollar bills. All hundreds.

"In case you needed anything," said Romi.

And now Karina was feeling like a whore again, despite the lack of physical contact.

"Thanks," she said, mustering a smile. "I'll just hang out here today."

She headed back up to her room, not really sure what she was going to do to keep busy. The sun was shining brightly outside the French doors, and she decided it would be a good day to try out the pool.

After changing and grabbing her cell phone and e-reader, she snaked through the kitchen on her way to the pool. Romi was nowhere to be found, but Karina managed to scrounge up some fruit and a bottle of water without any help.

Once she was settled on a chair, she called Ginny again and was surprised when she picked up.

"About damn time," Ginny said. "I was starting to get worried."

"I left you a voicemail. And why aren't you working?"

"I am. I happened to be in the back when I heard my phone ring. I only have a couple minutes, so talk fast. Are you okay?"

"I'm fine," Karina said. "More than fine. Nothing has happened."

"What do you mean?"

"I mean the man has barely touched me. Hell, I feel like I've barely seen him. He's out of town now and isn't supposed to be back until tomorrow."

"Weird," said Ginny.

"I know. The whole thing doesn't make any sense. Why would he go through all this trouble?"

"I don't know. Maybe—shoot I have to go. Talk to you soon."

"Okay," Karina said and hung up. "Thanks for nothing," she muttered to herself.

By the next day, Karina was absolutely stir-crazy and finally had Romi arrange a car for her. She just wanted to be taken to a beach, somewhere she could stretch her legs, and the driver was more than obliging, but she felt uncomfortable being driven around. And it was even more awkward to have someone waiting for her as she walked around doing nothing. In the end, she was barely gone an hour.

Romi prepared a dinner for Karina and she ate it at one of the outdoor tables, but there was still no sign of Damien when she dropped her empty plate in the sink.

That evening, she tossed and turned from too much unspent energy. Boredom was the last thing she had expected during the journey here.

By half past eleven she was lying on her side, watching the two little dots on the bedside clock flash, wondering if they had a name. Had she ever known and just forgot it along with all the other useless information she failed to recall?

There was a noise downstairs, and Karina sat up. It must be Damien, she thought. She pulled on a robe and headed out to the hall. As she approached the top of the stairs, she heard his voice.

"Thank you," he said. "That'll be all for tonight."

She waited to see if he would come up the stairs, but his footsteps disappeared. Quietly, she descended and could see light spilling into the foyer from the sitting room. She heard a clink as she neared the bottom. Peeking into the room, she found Damien stretched out in a chair, his eyes closed and a tumbler in one of his hands.

He hadn't seen her. She should climb back up to her room.

"Did I wake you?" he asked without opening his eyes.

Karina looked around, expecting it to be someone else he was talking to. But then he opened his eyes and there was no surprise when he focused on her.

"I couldn't sleep," she said.

"Help yourself to a night cap," he said, gesturing to the mini bar next to him.

"You look tired," she said as she stepped into the room.

"I just lost twenty-five million dollars on a deal that fell through."

"I'm sorry."

He shrugged. "I'll make it up. But I hate wasting my time on something that was never going to happen."

"Oh."

"So are you going to have one?" he asked.

"Um, sure."

She made her way to the bar, and as she walked past Damien, she felt something brush against her hand. She looked down just in time to see his hand lay back down on the arm of the chair, and his eyes were closed again.

Her hand shook as she pulled the top off a decanter—that was the clink she heard—and poured herself a glass of something. She held the glass to her lips, thinking of his fingers grazing her. It was the simplest touch, but it was enough to let loose the butterflies. Yet there was no sick feeling this time.

She gulped the warm liquor in one take, trying to quell the damn winged creatures.

"I'd appreciate it if you didn't shoot my two-hundred-dollar cognac."

She glanced at him to see that his eyes were open again, watching her.

"Sorry," she said, putting the glass down and moving over to the couch across from him. She settled into the corner of it, finding it to be almost as comfortable as her bed upstairs. "In all fairness though, it's not like you can't afford a hundred more bottles."

"True," he sighed. "But I buy it to enjoy, to savor. Not to kill brain cells in the quickest manner. And you might not want a repeat of your first night here."

Karina felt the heat rise to her cheeks. Damien was still watching her, and she forced herself to look at something else.

"So is the piano here just for show, or can you actually play it?"

He set his tumbler down and pushed himself up out of the chair. There was a cover over the keys that he lifted and slid back before sitting on the bench.

"Any special requests?" he asked.

"Impress me."

His fingers did a little dance over the keys, warming up, and then he started playing a slow, haunting tune.

"Mmm…. Moonlight Sonata," she said, curling into a ball. "I've always loved that song, even though it sounds so sad."

"You know your Beethoven."

She crinkled her nose. "Any kid that did junior high band or orchestra knows Moonlight Sonata."

"And were you in band or orchestra?"

"I was," she said, closing her eyes. The cognac and piano were working together to finally relax her.

"Let me guess," he said. "You played the clarinet."

"The cello."

"Really? Were you any good?" he asked.

"I was decent."

"Do you still play?"

"No," she said. "I played up until my freshman year of college to get the arts requirement out of the way. But there wasn't much point in continuing if I wasn't going to major in it." She frowned, eyes still closed. "When my mom got sick, I convinced them to sell it to help pay the bills and that was that."

"How sad," he said.

"The thing was just gathering dust anyway."

No one said anything else as the song ended and he moved right into another piece just as beautiful and soothing, and Karina was content to simply lie there, listening to him play.

Come Undone

KARINA WOKE WITH a start to realize that she was still on the couch, but Damien was gone and all the lights were off. She sat up, and a throw blanket fell down around her waist. Cautiously, she found her way back upstairs, where she paused at her bedroom door, looking down the hall at Damien's door. She tiptoed toward it. Placing a hand against the door, she listened, but nothing could be heard. She carefully pressed down his handle, expecting it to be locked, but it wasn't. Holding her breath, she guided it back up before rushing back to her room and burrowing under her covers. What did it matter that his door wasn't locked? What had even possessed her to go to it?

The next morning, Karina came downstairs to find Damien at the dining table, reading something on an iPad. There was a variety of breakfast items laid out on the table.

"Breakfast wasn't nearly this fancy with you gone,"

Karina said as she sat down at the only other place setting.

Damien looked up with a frown. "You should've asked," he said.

"I was only teasing," she said, spooning some scrambled eggs onto her plate. "It wouldn't have been necessary."

"I have to attend a party this evening. I was hoping you would join me."

Karina paused mid-bite.

"You mean it's not mandatory?" she asked.

"You think I would force you to come?" He narrowed his eyes at her.

"I, well, I suppose not."

"Does that mean you'd rather stay home tonight?"

Karina didn't even have to think about the answer to that.

"Getting out of the house sounds like a great idea."

"Good. The car will be here by seven-thirty, so make sure you're ready by then."

He pulled a napkin from his lap and stood.

"Where are you going?" she asked.

"I have work to do. But I'll just be in my office if you need anything."

He disappeared, leaving Karina to breakfast by herself. What could she possibly need from him? Maybe some attention, perhaps? The last thought shocked her. It was the boredom speaking. Getting out tonight would do her some good.

Karina wasn't exactly sure what to wear for the party, but judging by the way Damien dressed just for dinner in his own home, she was going to go out on a limb and say the attire wasn't casual. Since he hadn't given any direction, she hoped she wasn't breaking any rules when she chose a knee-length Diane von Furstenberg wrap dress covered in black lace.

At a quarter after seven, she headed down to find Damien in the sitting room again, enjoying a drink. He was dressed in an understated black suit over a crisp white shirt and no tie.

His face lit up as she walked into the room, and Karina felt a slight flutter in her chest.

"Excellent choice," he said. "Would you care for something before we leave?"

She nodded and he poured. This time she made sure to savor it.

"You'll need to be careful with the wrap-dress though," he said as he replaced the stopper on the decanter.

"Why is that?" she asked, worried.

"Because one little tug and you'll come undone." He stared at her over the glass as he took a sip, and Karina couldn't look away.

A car could be heard pulling up, and Damien finally released her from his gaze. He escorted her to the vehicle, and together they rode to the party that turned out to be at a house only a couple blocks away.

"We could've just walked here," she whispered as they climbed the steps to a mansion almost as impressive as Damien's.

"You don't walk this neighborhood," he whispered back.

"So I've heard," she muttered.

An hour into the party, Karina began to wonder if maybe she would have been better off spending another evening alone at the house. The event was an engagement party for the hostess' daughter, and everyone kept telling Damien how honored they were that he was able to attend. At least all the women did. He paid more attention to one well-wisher in the five minutes they chatted than he had to Karina her entire time in Miami so far.

A waiter walked by with a tray of champagne and she snagged one, trying to figure out why it bothered her so much. It didn't help that Damien rarely introduced her. Only when someone asked did he introduce her simply as Karina Watson. Although to be honest, she didn't know what he was supposed to call her. Date, maybe?

And then *she* arrived.

"Damien!" she gushed, holding her arms out as she approached him.

"Tabitha," he said with a big smile as she embraced him.

Karina swapped her empty champagne glass for a fresh one as she watched Damien kiss her cheek.

"I didn't realize you were back in town," he said.

"Just flew in this morning. Can't you tell by how jet-lagged I am?"

"I'd never guess," he replied. "You look flawless as ever."

"Oh, stop," she laughed, giving him a gentle push on the chest.

Karina had to agree with Damien. Not a single golden hair on Tabitha's blonde head was out of place, and her skin was luminescent. It was disgusting.

Tabitha leaned in close to Damien and whispered something in his ear. He was looking right at Karina, but she could tell he wasn't really seeing her. She looked down to see his hand on her waist and felt something twist inside of her. But then he threw his head back, laughing at whatever Tabitha had said, and the hand moved away.

It was too much. Karina set her champagne glass on a nearby table and walked up to Damien. Tabitha gave her only a brief glance. She knew that Karina wasn't a threat.

"May I talk to you for a second?" Karina asked.

"Of course," he said. "Tabitha, will you excuse us?"

"Don't be long," Tabitha said with a flip of her hair.

Karina fought the urge to gag as she led Damien to a quiet corner.

"Is everything okay?" he asked. And here was serious Damien again. Not the animated one who had been laughing with everyone else all night.

"Are you—are you sleeping with her?" she asked point blank.

"Tabitha? God no!"

"Why did you even ask me to come? I'm starting to feel like a third wheel."

He placed a hand against the wall behind her and leaned in close.

"Are you jealous?" he asked quietly.

"What? No! That's ridiculous."

"Then what's the problem here?"

"It's just…it's just that…." And then the words slipped out before she could even think about it. "I thought *I* was the one you wanted."

A small, dangerous smile started to spread across his face, and Karina was sure he was going to kiss her. But then he stood, letting his arm drop back down to his side.

"We should head home," he said. "I think I've had about enough of these people."

Karina frowned and followed him to the front door without him saying so much as a goodbye to anyone. They found their driver and the car was brought around. As the car pulled away, Damien rested a hand on her knee. Karina waited for it to move higher up, even found herself wanting it to. But it remained in the same spot until the car stopped in front of his house, and he removed it before helping her out of the vehicle. She felt his hand on the small of her back as they walked to the front door, but that disappeared as well when they walked inside.

She stood in the foyer, waiting for him to say something, except that he started climbing the steps without saying anything.

"Where are you going?" she called out.

He stopped and turned around. "I'm going to bed. Unless you need anything."

"No," she said, disappointed. "Good night then."

"Good night, Karina." And he continued up the stairs.

After he disappeared from view, she made her own trek upstairs and dressed for bed. This time she bypassed her familiar leggings and opted for a black lace chemise, courtesy of Damien Bishop. She assumed this was one of the pieces he had personally requested. But why, she wondered as she stood in front of the mirror, admiring the way it hugged her slender body. It couldn't possibly be only for her personal enjoyment. Deciding it was time for some answers, she walked out of her bedroom and approached Damien's door.

She knocked a couple times, but there was no answer. She tried the handle and found that it opened just as easily as the night before. Worried that he might be asleep already, she gently pushed the door open, but the sound of running water explained why he had not answered her knocks.

The door to his bathroom was open, and she walked toward it just as the water shut off. She froze, trying to decide what to do. And then he stepped out of the shower, grabbing a nearby towel. He rubbed it through his hair, and since he was facing the mirror, Karina knew she still had one chance to walk away. But he turned before she did, and now she was caught.

"Can I help you?" he asked, tossing the towel over his shoulder

She now had a full view of his front and discovered that his chest was just as ripped as his back, his broad torso creating a V that drew her eyes right down to—good god, even slack it was impressive.

"Was there something that you needed?" he asked and she swallowed, trying to find her tongue.

"Why haven't you had sex with me yet?" she asked, taking a step toward him.

"Why?" He had the same smile from the party. "Do you want me to?"

"What!" she exclaimed. "Of course not."

"I don't believe you," he said, closing the gap between them.

"Well, it's the truth."

Suddenly he grabbed her arm and pulled her toward him before pushing her against the counter so that she was facing the mirror, his chest pressed against her back. Water from his body soaked though her lingerie as his hands trapped hers against the granite.

"You're lying," he murmured into her ear. "And I can prove it."

"How?" she breathed.

He grasped her right hand and forced it to her leg.

"I'm willing to bet my entire fortune," he said, kissing the top of her ear, "that you're wet right now."

Karina said nothing—how could she argue—as he slid the hand up under her chemise and managed to slip both hands in her underwear. She bit her tongue, stifling a moan.

"What do you feel?" he asked.

"Nothing," she whispered and he bit into her shoulder.

"You're lying again."

His finger began rubbing her ever so gently, and she managed to pull her hand free, placing it back on the counter.

"Do you want to know why I haven't had sex with you yet?" he asked, looking at her through the mirror. She could only nod. "Because only a desperate man takes something. A wiser, more patient man waits for it to come to him."

And then he plunged a finger deep inside of her and she thought her knees would give out.

"See that face," he whispered into her ear.

Karina looked at the woman staring back at her. The flushed skin, the bright blue eyes. Even her lips, almost forming a perfect O, were redder, fuller than usual. She hardly recognized herself.

"I get off every night just imagining that look on your face."

Damien pulled his hand away and stepped back. Karina caught herself against the counter before her legs buckled.

"It's time for bed," he said, and Karina turned unsteadily to face him.

"The question is will you be climbing into my bed? Or your own?"

The towel had fallen to the floor, and he now stood before her in all his naked glory. She locked eyes with him, ignoring the erection slowly building as they stared each other down.

Karina wanted him more than she'd thought possible. But now that she knew the game he was playing, she refused to give him the satisfaction. Instead, she slowly turned toward the door and walked away. He said nothing as she walked out of the room, slamming the door behind her.

She plopped onto her bed and pulled the covers up over her head, cursing Damien Bishop. Her body throbbed where he had touched her, desperate for relief. She tried to take care of it herself, but it just wasn't the same and she eventually had to give up, crying out in frustration.

Game On

THE SUN SHONE brightly into Karina's room when she woke the next morning, but it did nothing to improve her mood. She couldn't shake the feeling of irritation...of frustration. Damien had made one mistake, though. He had shown his hand too soon. And he had no idea who he was messing with.

She headed downstairs only to find that Damien wasn't even home.

"He had to go into the main office," Romi told her.

"Do you know when he'll be back?" Karina asked.

Romi shook her head. "He didn't say, and with Mr. Bishop you never know."

After breakfast, she went upstairs to call her parents (Miami is great, haven't had a chance to see much since she had been working so hard) and Ginny, who she lied to as well.

"Still nothing?" Ginny asked.

"Nope."

"Maybe he's gay and wants you around to make the press think that he's straight."

"Maybe," said Karina.

"Well at least you get to enjoy a free vacation out of it."

"That is a plus."

"Enjoy it," said Ginny. "The weather here is awful."

"I'll do my best."

"I miss you! It's so lonely here without you."

"Miss you too. Talk to you soon."

Karina went downstairs to make herself a sandwich for lunch and then decided she needed to listen to Ginny's advice and enjoy the Miami sun.

After a couple laps in the pool, she let herself dry in the sun before applying some sunscreen and starting another book on her e-reader. It wasn't as good as she had hoped (or perhaps she had too many other things on her mind), so after the second chapter she shut it off and popped in some ear buds instead.

She closed her eyes and let the sun's warmth blanket her. It was so relaxing, she just might fall asleep. Lazily, she wondered if she should apply more sunscreen, just in case….

A shadow blocked the light and she opened her eyes to see Damien standing over her. She pulled the buds from her ears.

"You're home," she said.

"Enjoying yourself?" he asked, hands in his trouser pockets.

"Is there something else you'd rather I be doing?" she asked slyly.

Instead of answering, he just looked at her with the familiar hunger.

Yesterday she would've cringed under that gaze, maybe even covered herself with the towel. But not today. Today it was time to even the playing field.

Karina let out a contented sigh as she raised her arms above her head and stretched. She could almost see the fire in his eyes.

"Get dressed," he said as he turned around—much to her disappointment—and walked away. "I'm taking you to dinner."

"What should I wear?" she called out.

"Whatever you want," he said over his shoulder.

Game on.

After a shower, Karina perused the closet, looking for just the right outfit. Her first instinct was to go for the shortest, skimpiest thing that she could find, but then decided that was too obvious. She needed something more subtle. And she found it in a strapless maxi dress. The tag said cotton, but something about the weave or wash made it feel like butter against her skin. Tom sure knew how to shop.

When she came down the stairs, Damien was waiting for her by the door, impatiently tapping a long blue box against his hand. But he stopped as soon as he saw her, and Karina knew she had chosen the right dress. Not that he was any less impressive in his fitted light gray slacks and yet another button-down shirt, this time in black. And now she knew exactly what the shirt was covering. This was not going to be easy.

"Are you ready?" he asked and she nodded. "I have something for you."

He held out the box and opened it for her. Inside was a necklace—a thin silver chain with three small, sparkling diamonds spaced out on the front of it.

She didn't know what to say. No man had ever given her jewelry before, let alone something from Tiffany's.

"It's too much," she said. "I can't accept this."

"Consider it a loan," he told her. "You can leave it behind when you leave, if you want."

"For the next girl."

"That's a thought," he said with a smirk.

Even though she was sure he was joking, Karina felt an odd twinge of jealousy.

"Let me," he said, pulling the necklace from the box.

She turned around and held her hair up so the he could clasp it around her neck. It seemed to take longer than she thought necessary, and when he finally finished, he ran a hand down the length of her bared back, sending a shiver through her that he must have noticed.

"Thank you," she whispered, turning to face him again.

He offered his arm, giving her a warm smile. "Shall we?" he asked.

She looped her hand through it, and together they walked out and down the steps to where a Porsche convertible was waiting instead of the town car Karina had been expecting.

"No driver tonight?" she asked as he held the passenger door open for her.

"I thought tonight could be just the two of us." He closed her door and got into the driver's seat.

"I was beginning to think you didn't have a driver's license."

He started the engine.

"You might not believe that I do after tonight," he said and tore off down the driveway, making her laugh.

They managed to arrive at the restaurant in one piece, if only because traffic slowed considerably as they got near the heart of Miami. Once again, Karina was amazed at all the colors and nightlife attire.

"Is this typical for a Friday night?" she asked.

"This is typical every night. *Esto es Miami*. We like to

party."

"Do *you* like to party?" she asked, raising an eyebrow at him. Because nothing she had seen so far suggested he was into clubbing.

He shrugged. "When the occasion arises. It's not really my scene."

Damien pulled up to a Cuban restaurant across the street from the beach and let the valet handle the parking.

There was a line waiting at the hostess booth, but Damien walked right up and shook the hostess' hand.

"I called earlier today about a table on the balcony."

As he released her hand, Karina noticed the hostess had something wadded in it.

"Of course, right this way."

She led them through the crowded dining room and out to the equally crowded balcony where their table had a perfect view of the action.

"Your server should be right with you," the hostess said and walked away.

"You didn't call earlier today, did you?" Karina asked.

"I did," he said, focusing on the menu. "They told me their reservations were full for the weekend."

"Yet here we are."

"Here we are," he said, and there was a glimmer in his eye as he looked up at her.

"I have to say I'm surprised that you're venturing out sans bodyguards."

"It draws less attention when I'm trying to be inconspicuous," he said. "I can assure you though that they're nearby. Just in case something goes wrong."

"And has it?" she asked. "Has anything ever gone wrong?"

His brow furrowed and his eyes went dark. "Once," he said without offering any further explanation. "Have you ever had Cuban food before?" he asked, changing the subject as he turned his gaze back to the menu.

"Does rum count?"

"I don't think so," he said with a smile.

"Then tonight will be a first."

"We should try a rum flight while we're here as well."

"What's a rum flight?" she asked.

"It's like a wine flight. Only with rum."

She continued to look at him.

"It's a sampling of various rums to try."

"Why? Rum is rum. How different can it be?" she asked.

"We will definitely be ordering a rum flight then."

"It will probably be wasted on me."

"We shall see," he said. "And tomorrow I think we will be visiting a wine bar."

"I can't wait," she said with a smile as the server arrived.

Karina let Damien order for the both of them, since she had no idea where to start. She wasn't even sure how to pronounce half the items, and the words sounded so much sexier coming from his mouth.

"Let's start with *frituras de malanga* and…" he looked at Karina. "You like calamari, don't you?"

"Isn't that squid?" she asked, wrinkling her nose.

"So you've tried it then?"

"Well, no," she admitted.

"We'll take some calamari," he told their waitress, who nodded. "And for dinner," he said, turning back to the menu. "We'll try the *ropa vieja,* and bring a side of black bean soup."

"Of course," she said, collecting their menus.

"Do I want to know what you just ordered?" Karina asked.

"I promise it's nothing too exotic," he said.

"You ordered squid."

"Promise me you'll keep an open mind. The calamari here is amazing. My favorite, in fact."

She folded her arms, leaning forward on the table. "Tonight is going to be full of firsts for me, isn't it?"

He gave a sly grin. "We can only hope."

The rum flight arrived first, and Damien gave her a lesson on how to try them.

"You start down here with the lightest one," he said, pointing to the first of the four glasses on the small, wooden platter between them, all slightly smaller than a shot glass. "And you sip it. You don't want to finish it all at once."

"Why not?" she asked.

"Because after you try a little of each, you can go back and compare your favorites."

"What are you going to drink?"

"Very funny," he said with a half-cocked smile. "I'm pretty sure we've established what a lightweight you are."

Karina blushed as she picked up the first glass and took a small sip. There was the familiar burn of straight alcohol, but it actually had a nice flavor to it.

"I think I like that," she said, handing the glass to Damien. Their fingers touched as he took it, and she tried to ignore the tingling it caused.

"Not bad," he said after taking a sip. "A little weak."

She moved on to the next one. "Oh, I really like that one." This time she set the glass down and opted to push it toward him before moving on to the next one, which was much darker and far too strong for her.

"Oh god," she said as she winced from the potency of it.

Damien broke out in laughter over her reaction, causing her to blush again. He wrapped his fingers around her hand still holding the glass and pulled it toward his mouth, taking a sip.

"Now *that* I like," he said, releasing her. "That's a good one."

She pushed the last one in his direction.

"You're not done, are you?" he asked.

"You taste it," she said, pointing to it. "Tell me if you think I'll like it."

Damien took her hand again and this time dipped her finger in it before slowly sucking the rum off. Karina's whole body trembled.

"You're right," he said, letting go of her hand. "I think this one is much too strong for you. You wouldn't be able to handle it."

She pulled the glass back and looked him in the eye before drinking half of it. She forced herself not to shudder as it burned its way down her throat.

"Bolder than I'm used to, but nothing I can't handle."

He lifted one of the other rums. "A toast, then?"

"Oh, now we're shooting them?"

He shrugged. "Rules were meant to be broken."

Karina held her half glass up to his almost full one.

"To a beautiful evening," he said. "With beautiful company."

"Cheers," she said, clinking her glass against his before downing the drink.

Dinner was amazing—including the calamari, much to Karina's surprise. She was enjoying the last sips of her equally delicious mojito when music began blaring from inside the restaurant. She craned her neck to see people moving out onto a dance floor in the back bar area.

"Looks like the salsa dancing is starting," said Damien.

"How fun," she muttered, watching some of the dancers.

"Have you ever tried it?" he asked and she shook her head. "Would you like to?"

"Oh no," she said, turning back to her drink. "I think I would step on too many toes."

To her dismay, he stood and held out his hand.

"We'll never know for sure if you don't try," he said.

Karina bit her lip. She also didn't know if she could handle being that close to his body. Wasn't salsa dancing supposed to be…intimate?

"All right," she whispered, taking his hand as she stood.

Together they weaved through the crowd and staked out a spot on the dance floor.

"You realize I don't know the first thing about salsa dancing," she said as he placed a warm hand on her waist. "I'm not even that good of a dancer in general."

"Just follow my lead and you'll be fine," he said into her ear so she could hear him over the Latin beat pumping through the speakers. "And make sure to move your hips a lot. No one will know the difference."

She took a deep breath and did her best, but the steps were so fast and there were so many people around them. People who actually knew what they were doing.

Every time she tripped into him, however, he only laughed, and she couldn't help laughing with him, wondering if he was enjoying her lack of ability.

"You're right," he chuckled into her ear as he pulled her closer, forcing her hips to keep time with his. "You're terrible at this!"

"I told you," she said, giggling. Because while it was true, she was still having fun. She couldn't remember the last time she had laughed so hard. And even though she continued to step on his feet—just as she had predicted—he never complained, just kept leading her, spinning her, until she finally managed to find the rhythm.

"*Muy bien*," he said after twirling her back into his arms. Their faces, their lips were so close now. "You're getting the hang of it," he said, his voice gravelly.

All either of them had to do was lean in only a fraction of an inch more….

Someone bumped hard into Damien, breaking their embrace.

"*Lo sieto*," said a male dancer with an apologetic smile.

"*No hay problema*," Damien replied with a half-smile. He leaned back into Karina, his lips close to her ear again. "It think it's getting a little crowded. Shall we head home?"

She nodded, feeling the familiar butterflies in her stomach, and he laced his fingers through hers before carving a path off the dance floor.

Restraint

THE DRIVE HOME was just as quiet as the drive there, but whenever he wasn't shifting, Damien rested his hand on Karina's left knee. She watched the scenery go by, pretending it was nothing to have him touch her, when really she couldn't stop imaging what that hand had done to her just last night, even though neither of them had mentioned it.

Eventually they were pulling up to the house, and Damien drove into the garage, where she discovered it wasn't his only toy on four wheels.

"How do you decide which one to drive?" she asked as he helped her out of the car.

"Depends on what mood I'm in." He placed his hand on the small of her back as they walked into the house.

"And what kind of mood were you in when you chose the Porsche?"

"I've always thought of the 911 as playful yet

seductive," he said with a devilish grin.

This time, he kept his hand on her back the entire walk up the stairs, only releasing it when they reached her bedroom.

"I really enjoyed myself," she said, leaning her back against the door.

"I'm happy to hear that," he said, bracing a hand just above her shoulder, moving in close until there was only a hair's width between them.

She waited for the kiss, her heart racing in anticipation of it.

"I suppose this is where we say good-night," he whispered.

"Are you sure?" she asked demurely.

His eyes searched her face, finally focusing on her lips.

"Unless perhaps you'd like to join me in my room tonight."

She took a deep breath, causing her chest to swell until it was touching him. "Mmm…I think I'll stay in my bed tonight."

He ran a thumb down her cheek and brushed it against her lips.

"Suit yourself," he said, pushing off the wall and walking toward his room.

Katrina tried to control her breathing, impressed—and frustrated—with the man's restraint. She was beginning to wonder if she could win this war.

She had a hard time falling asleep that night, fighting the urge to slink off into his room. The only comfort was knowing that he was in the same boat, for there had been no mistaking the hard-on straining against her earlier.

Karina woke to shouting the next morning and realized it was Damien outside. She pulled a silk robe around her and went out to the balcony, looking around until she found him on the sailboat at the edge of the property. Wearing nothing but shorts, he was shouting to whoever was helping him. She rested on her forearms, taking pleasure in watching him work as he threw ropes about.

Eventually he caught sight of her and gave a wave.

"Oh, Karina," he said as though calling up to Juliet. "I'm taking the boat out today. Care to join me?"

"I would be delighted to," she called back.

"Hurry down then," he said. "The day is wasting away!"

Karina raced back into the room and pulled on a bikini, then slipped a tank top over it before wrapping a sarong around her waist. She stepped into some flip flops and then rushed down and out to the boat. She walked across the dock and let Damien help her climb on board, where she fell against his warm torso.

"Might take a minute to get your sea legs," he said with a smile as he helped her stand up straight. "Go ahead and sit for a minute while I get us out of here."

There weren't exactly any seats up top, so she just tried to find the safest place to plant her bottom. She pulled her hair up into a ponytail as she waited. It was bound to be windy.

The young man who had been helping remained on the dock, watching as Damien expertly guided the craft out into the open water using an outboard motor. Once they were far enough away from shore, Damien gave the man a wave.

"I'll call when we're on our way back," he shouted.

"Anything I can do to help?" Karina offered.

He looked at her and frowned.

"What's wrong?" she asked.

"It's your shoes. I didn't think to check before you climbed aboard."

"Why?

"Flip flops are the last thing you want to wear on a boat," he said.

"Should I take them off?"

"It's your toes I'm worried about. But you should probably take them off anyway. There's also the risk of spraining your ankle if the boat lurches and you instinctively try to keep the shoe on."

Karina pulled them off and set them aside.

"Sorry," she said. "It's my first time on a sailboat."

"Do you still want to help?" he asked.

"Of course."

With Damien's direction, Karina helped get the sail up and pointed in the right direction. It wasn't long before they were pulling even farther away from the shore, and there was nothing left for her to do while he steered.

"Would you like to take the helm?" he asked.

"You trust me with your boat?"

"It's not like I won't be right here." He scanned the horizon. "And I don't think I need to worry about you running us into anything."

Karina rubbed her hands together as she stepped in next to him. She was shocked to discover it was nothing like steering a car. The wheel pulled as soon as she took hold, and Damien grabbed it quickly before it could make a full rotation, spinning it back into position.

"The ocean wants to pull you with it," he said, positioning himself behind her so they could both hold the wheel. "But you can't let it. You have to be stronger than her."

"What happens if you're not?" she asked, feeling his chest rise against her with each steady breath.

"Then she'll eat you alive," he said in a low voice, his breath hot against her ear, and a shiver swept through her body.

Eventually Karina got the hang of it and Damien slowly

pulled his hands away.

"You got it?"

She nodded, fully aware that she was grinning like a fool. She was sailing a boat in the Atlantic. Granted they were still close enough to see the Miami skyline, but that didn't make it any less exhilarating.

"Be right back, then," he said and her grin disappeared. "I'm not going far," he said with a laugh. She watched him disappear below deck and come back up a few minutes later with a basket. He set it down near a railing and started dropping the sails.

"There's a blanket in that box over there," he said as he locked the steering wheel.

Karina found it and he helped her lay it out on the large flat area at the bow of the boat. She kneeled on the blanket as he handed her a glass from the basket and then pulled a small bottle of white wine from it. Just enough for the two of them.

"You weren't planning on sailing alone today, were you?" she asked as he filled her glass.

"I'm pretty sure you know the answer to that," he said, pouring into his glass before raising it. "*Salut*?"

"*Salut*," she said, tapping her glass to his.

She took a sip and Damien laid out on his side next to her, leaning on his elbow.

A strand of hair had escaped her ponytail, and she pushed it out of her face. "Is it always this gorgeous here? Year-round, I mean."

He took a long swig before answering. "It gets pretty hot in the summer—well into the hundreds. And it's even more humid."

"That's hard to believe," she said.

"But yes, the weather is pretty nice twelve months out of the year."

She looked out over the horizon to where the sparkling

water met the bright blue sky. "Doesn't it ever rain?" she asked.

"It rains pretty often, mostly in summer," he said, placing his empty glass into the basket. "It usually only lasts an hour or so. And even that is warm."

"What about hurricanes?" she asked. "I know you get those."

"Are we really so boring that we're sitting in the middle of the ocean on a beautiful day discussing the weather?"

Karina finished the last drop of her wine and put her glass in with Damien's before lying so that she was facing him, resting her head in her palm. "What would you rather talk about then?"

"How about," he pushed the wild strand back behind her ear, "we discuss why you won't come to my bed?"

She felt the heat rising to her cheeks. "Probably for the same reason you won't come to mine," she said.

He traced a finger along the length of her arm right down to the hand resting on her leg. "And what reason is that?" he asked.

She moved her hand, planting it in front of her, but the plan backfired—his palm simply remained on her thigh with only the thin sarong between it and her flesh.

"Because we're both stubborn," she said.

"Hmm. So you're saying we're at a stalemate then?"

"Afraid so."

He scooted an inch closer. "But what if," his hand slid down to the off-centered knot at her waist, "we were on neutral ground?" His fingers started to work at the knot. "Say, on a boat in the middle of the ocean."

He leaned forward and kissed her neck. She closed her eyes just as the knot came undone. He leaned back and glided the sarong down her leg, leaving goosebumps in its wake.

"Are you surrendering then?" she asked, opening her

eyes to see that hungry look again. When did it become such a turn-on?

"I didn't say that. But I don't think you want me to stop."

"Perhaps I do."

He leaned into her again, moving his hand to the top of her thigh, his thumb resting on the front of her bikini bottom. "We both know I can tell when you're lying," he whispered into her ear, and she placed a hand on his chest, sinking her nails into him. He was right. She no longer cared about winning this game.

And then a phone started ringing and Damien pulled back, frowning.

"Tom was only supposed to call in an emergency," he said, standing up.

Karina rolled onto her back, cursing Tom. Couldn't he have waited another twenty minutes? She closed her eyes, imagining his hands on her again. Okay, maybe an hour.

It was too windy to hear his words from the back of the boat as she lay there, but he definitely sounded agitated.

A couple minutes later, Damien was raising the sails.

"Is everything all right?" she asked, sitting up.

"We have to head back." His tone was curt, and it was hard to tell if he was mad at her or whatever Tom had said.

She folded the blanket and tucked it away before taking the basket down below. By the time she came back up, they were already sailing in a straight line back to his property. All the playfulness had left the air, and Damien only spoke to her when he needed help with the rigging.

There were two men when they got back to the house this time, and as soon as Damien had helped her safely onto the dock, he headed toward the house, leaving the two men to take care of the boat. Not sure what else to do, she followed him inside, where they were immediately met by Tom.

"I've already packed your bags, and Jim is getting the plane ready as we speak," he said, keeping step with Damien, who continued through the house and up the stairs. "The car should be here in twenty minutes at the most. I hope that gives you enough time."

"I just need a quick shower." Damien said.

"Where are you going?" Karina called out from the bottom step.

Both men stopped walking and turned to face her as though they'd forgotten all about her. Damien came back down.

"There's been an emergency shareholder's meeting called in Beijing. A completely bullshit meeting, but it's imperative that I'm there to keep things from getting any worse."

"How long will you be gone?" she asked. She realized she didn't want him to go. She wanted him to stay here, with her, to take her back out on the boat.

"I don't know. Only a couple days, hopefully. A week at the most."

"A *week*." That was almost a quarter of the time she was supposed to be here. Five days ago she would have been breathing a sigh of relief. But now….

"I'm sorry," he said, kissing her cheek. And then he rushed back up the stairs to Tom, who kept talking to him as they walked away.

Doubts

KARINA HAD NEVER known boredom like this before. And she never imagined it could've come while in a house as impressive as Damien's. The truth was that she missed him more than she wanted to admit. Something had changed, a shift had occurred, and once the walls had come down, it turned out she enjoyed his company—even when he wasn't touching her (though she rather preferred that part).

Monday morning she was curled up on a lounge chair, watching the filter robot moving along the bottom of the pool. She wondered if there was a pattern, or if the movements really were random. What if it kept missing the same spot?

Annoyed with herself, she stood up just as Romi came out holding a phone.

"It's Mr. Bishop for you," she said.

Karina's heart raced at the thought of hearing his voice.

"Hello," she said.

"Bored yet?" he asked.

"I'm keeping busy," she lied. "Why? Are you heading home to come interrupt my fun?"

"Unfortunately not," he sighed. "Which is why I'm calling. I have to attend a charity event on Saturday."

"Will you be back in time?"

"I'd better be, I'm the keynote speaker. I was hoping you'd come with me."

She laughed. "You called from China just to ask me on a date?"

"Actually, I'm calling to tell you that you have an appointment tomorrow."

"I do?"

"Yes. Assuming you would agree to come, I made an appointment for a dress fitting. It's a formal affair. I had planned to take you to the fitting, but there's no way I'll be back in time, so I'm afraid you're on your own."

The idea didn't really appeal to her, at least not without Damien. It was something to kill the time though.

"I suppose I could fit it into my busy schedule," she said.

"It's at eleven, so you should leave by ten-thirty."

"You mean I get to drive one of your fancy cars?"

"Nice try," he said. "I've arranged a driver for you."

"Of course you did."

"And everything at the boutique has been taken care of. You don't need to worry about anything other than getting yourself there."

"Okay."

"I should probably get some sleep," he said. "The jet lag is killing me and I've got another long day tomorrow."

"All right," she said, sad to have to say to goodbye. "Good luck."

"And Karina?"

"Yes?"

"I'm sorry," he said. "The last thing I wanted to do was take off like this."

"It's fine," she told him. "Go get some sleep. I'll talk to you soon."

She hung up the phone. So tomorrow was planned for her, but that still left today to wallow in her boredom. Deciding she'd had enough of the sun, she ventured indoors to see what movies Damien kept stocked in that fancy entertainment room of his.

When Karina walked into the boutique the next day, she was painfully aware of how much she didn't belong here. Since she would just be trying on dresses, she had opted for jeans and a tank top—a decision she regretted as the three impeccably dressed women behind the counter glanced in her direction with a look of disapproval. Karina walked toward them, and the tallest of the three finally approached her.

"I'm sorry miss, but we're by appointment only," she said with a fake, condescending smile. Maybe Karina didn't really need to go to this affair after all.

"I have an appointment. I'm Karina Watson."

The woman raised an eyebrow, clearly not believing her.

"Damien Bishop arranged it," Karina told her.

Everyone's demeanor changed at the mention of his name, and Karina hated these women even more for it.

"Oh yes," said one of the ladies, a blonde. "We've been expecting you!"

The third girl ran off to the back room.

"I'm Yvette," said the blonde. "Right this way and we can get started."

Yvette led her to a chair with a side table, and the third girl came out of the back room carrying a tray with champagne in an ice bucket and a single flute glass. Karina was grateful as the woman poured it, because she had a feeling she was going to need alcohol to survive these vultures.

As Karina took her first sip, Yvette pulled out a rack already containing some dresses.

"Mr. Bishop told us a little about the event and your size, so we went ahead and pulled a few items to get started. But let us know if you're looking for something different."

Karina stood, still holding the glass, and looked over the selection. They were all gorgeous. But it didn't take long to find her favorite—a strapless satin-twill gown in midnight black with an off-center slit on the front.

"Can I try this one on?" she asked.

"Of course."

Yvette grabbed the dress and showed Karina to a dressing room. The second she stepped into it, she knew this was the one. It was less embellished, less flashy than the others, but sometimes less was more. The slit came half way up her thigh, and the back flared a bit just below her backside. A mermaid skirt, Yvette called it.

She walked out and stood on a little platform in front of several mirrors.

"Wow," said the brunette who had brought out the champagne. "That dress is perfect."

Karina did a little turn—being careful not to fall and embarrass herself—so she could see the whole dress. It *was* perfect. She was almost sad that Damien wasn't here to see it, then decided she'd rather spring this on him later. At home.

"I don't even think you'll need any alterations. You are planning to wear heels, aren't you?"

Karina nodded. She was now, apparently.

Just then, a chime went off, signaling that another

customer had walked in.

"Yoo hoo, anyone here?" called a voice that made Karina's skin crawl. *Tabitha.*

She walked back to where Karina and the women were, looking much more put together than Karina had when she walked in.

"Oh, Miss Rose!" Yvette exclaimed, jumping to attention. "We weren't expecting you today."

Tabitha removed her oversized sunglasses. "I was in the area," she said. "I thought I would check in on my dress. Oh, hello." She had finally noticed Karina "Haven't I seen you before?"

Karina stepped down from the platform. "The engagement party," she mumbled.

"That's right. I was talking to Damien, and then you apparently had something urgent to tell him."

Karina wasn't sure how to respond to this woman. If she had disliked her at the party, that was nothing compared to what she was feeling now.

"I think I've decided on this dress," she told Yvette.

"Excellent choice," said Yvette.

"That is a gorgeous dress," Tabitha chimed in. "What's the occasion?"

"Some charity event this Saturday. I'm going with Damien," she said, trying to gain the upper hand.

There was a flash of venom in Tabitha's eyes, but it was gone so quickly that Karina couldn't be sure she hadn't imagined it.

"Ugh," said Tabitha. "Is it that stupid museum fundraiser? I went with him last year and it was *so* boring. I'm glad he was smart enough not to ask me again this year. Better you than me," she said with a forced smile.

Karina could feel the heat rising to her cheeks.

"Oh look, Miss Rose," Yvette suddenly called out. "I've found your dress. Shall I get you a dressing room?"

Karina hadn't even realized Yvette had left the room but was grateful for the interruption.

"Lilly, will you take care of Miss Watson while I help Miss Rose?"

"Absolutely," the brunette said before turning to Karina. "If you want to change, I can bag the dress and ring you up."

Karina nodded, not trusting herself to speak.

After changing back into her dingy jeans, Karina waited at the counter while Lilly found the right garment bag for the dress. She ran it through the register, but as Damien had promised, everything had been arranged and Karina didn't even have to sign for anything. Lilly brought the bag around from behind the counter and handed it to Karina.

"Just between you and me," Lilly said quietly, "Mr. Bishop has never bought Tabitha a five-thousand-dollar Jason Wu gown."

The girl was trying to make Karina feel better, but her brain got stuck on the five grand part.

"Um, thank you," she said, and made her way outside, where the driver was waiting to take her back to Damien's home.

When Karina got home that afternoon, she fired up the laptop and did a search on Tabitha Rose. It didn't take long to find her. Apparently she was a model, though it looked like it was mostly local stuff. Her parents were donors for various organizations, so they must have money.

Karina added Damien's name in the search box with Tabitha's, and the first thing that popped up was a photo of the two of them from an event. She read the caption and her heart sank. She'd been hoping that Tabitha was lying, that Damien had not actually taken her anywhere, but here was the proof. She slammed the computer shut, not wanting to see anything else.

By that evening, Tabitha's words had replayed in Karina's mind a million times, and it sounded uglier each time. Tabitha was jealous, Karina kept trying to tell herself. But the truth was that Tabitha and Damien must have dated on some level. He claimed that they never slept together, but what reason did she have to believe him?

"Miss Watson?"

Romi's voice cut into Karina's thoughts, and she looked up from where she was reading—or rather attempting to read—on the couch in the sitting room.

"I'm heading out for the evening," she said. "Do you need anything else before I go?"

"No," Karina said, shaking her head. "Of course not. Good night." It was still so weird to have people waiting on her.

"I'll set the alarm before I go."

"Thanks, Romi." Then she thought of something. "Wait."

Romi turned around.

"May I ask you something?"

"Of course," said Romi.

"Has there ever been a—a mistress of the house?"

"No, only you."

"Me?" Karina frowned. "I hardly think I count."

Romi shrugged. "I was instructed to make sure you felt at home and that we all did as you asked. Same thing as far as I'm concerned."

"Did you think it was weird he was bringing me home, then?"

Romi sat on the edge of the other end of the couch, keeping her posture straight.

"Honestly, when I got word to prepare for your arrival, I was sure that some nasty woman had finally sunk her claws into him. Most of the staff and I were bracing for a real witch to come barging in those doors."

Karina's eyes went big.

"But that wasn't the case," Romi concluded, apparently not willing to say any more on the matter.

"So he hasn't brought other girlfriends around?" Karina asked.

"I'm not really comfortable discussing Mr. Bishop's private affairs."

"You're right," Karina said, shaking her head. "I'm sorry I put you on the spot like that. Forget I asked."

"No worries," she said, rising from the couch. "Good night, Miss Watson."

"Night, Romi."

Karina heard the beep and then the door closing behind Romi. And now she was all alone. Well, not completely alone. She knew that Damien had security patrolling the property twenty-four seven, even if no one was home. Being obscenely wealthy was starting to sound like a real chore.

She sighed, thinking she should head up to her room. All that was waiting for her up there, though, was another night of restless sleep. She closed the book she had borrowed from Damien's library, giving up on it, and looked at the mini bar. Perhaps she just needed to take a page from his playbook and enjoy a nightcap. She stood and looked at the collection of crystal decanters. None of them were labeled, and so she sniffed each bottle until she found one that appealed to her. She poured a little of it into a cut-glass tumbler and took a sip. It was almost like wine but had a brown tinge to it and was much sweeter.

Deciding it was just what she needed, she poured more into her glass and then slowly made her way up the stairs. She paused at her door and looked down to Damien's room, as she had a dozen times before. She walked over to it and tried the handle. It was unlocked as usual, and she crept in without turning on the light. She took another sip as she wandered around the room, looking for clues about just who Damien Bishop was. Beyond obnoxiously rich and sexy as hell, of course.

There weren't many clues to be had, though. Very few personal items were in sight, and she drew the line at opening any drawers. She flipped on the light in his closet and ran her fingers along the hanging clothes. Mostly suits, a lot of white dress shirts.

Finding just as little in here, she turned the closet light off and walked over to the bed. She sat down on the edge and polished off her glass. Damien was right, this was helping to relax her. She set the empty tumbler on the nightstand and noticed something propped up against the docking station. She looked closer and realized it was a business card.

As she picked it up, she wondered whose business was so important that he kept their card by his pillow. It was hard to read in the light streaming through his balcony doors, but she didn't have to because she recognized the giant green coffee bean on it. It was the card for her coffee shop.

Karina laid back on the bed, fingering the card. Why would he keep this? Why had Damien been so desperate to bring her down here? Was he so bored with his life that he thought it great sport to find someone so far removed from his world for him to seduce on his own territory?

She was reminded of the short story from high school where the wealthy hunter lures shipwrecked sailors to his island so that he can hunt them, having grown weary of hunting less intelligent animals. *The Dangerous Game,* she remembered as she rolled over onto Damien's pillow, smelling his aftershave on it. That's all she was to him. Game. Perhaps he had dated Tabitha before, but he had been bored by her and had gone searching for different prey.

Karina felt a tear on her cheek and was surprised by it. What did she care? What about this whole situation surprised her? As another tear slid down onto the pillow, she realized it was because she didn't care about winning or losing anymore. She was done with this game.

Forfeit

"WELL THIS IS a welcomed surprise."

Karina opened her eyes to see Damien's silhouette on the edge of the bed.

"What are you doing in my room?" she asked.

"I'm sorry, *your* room?"

She bolted upright. *Oh shit.*

"I'm so sorry," she said.

"Don't apologize," he said. "I couldn't have asked for a better homecoming."

"I couldn't sleep last night and thought a change of scenery might help."

"And so you settled on my bed?"

Karina blushed. How was she supposed to explain this?

"I'll go," she said, sliding in the direction opposite him.

"Wait," he said, grabbing her arm. "What's the hurry?"

"I shouldn't be here," she said, pulling her arm from him and scrambling out of the room.

"Karina!"

She ducked into her dark room and closed the door behind her, locking it before sliding down to the floor.

There was a knock and she jumped.

"Karina?" Damien called from the other side.

She didn't answer, and he tried the handle that wouldn't turn.

"Karina, is something wrong?" he asked.

"Nothing," she said. "I promise I didn't snoop through anything."

"I didn't think you did. Will you please let me in and talk to me?"

"I'm too tired. Can we talk in the morning?"

She heard him sigh.

"Of course," he said, and then she heard his footstep disappear down the hall.

When she was sure he was gone, she climbed into bed, reading three a.m. on the clock, and fell into yet another fitful sleep. She really missed her own bed.

When Karina came down for breakfast the next morning, the usual fare was laid out, but no one was at the table and only her place setting was left.

"Where's Damien?" she asked Romi.

"He's already eaten. He's in his office now."

Karina wondered how the man found the energy as she headed to his home office and knocked on the door.

"Come in," he said briskly.

She opened the door and peeked in to see him staring at his laptop as he typed. His face brightened when he finally looked up.

"Karina."

"Can I talk to you?" she asked.

"Of course."

He closed his laptop and she walked over to sit on the

corner of his desk.

"Is everything okay?" he asked, looking concerned.

She looked down at her hands, unable to face him.

"The deal was thirty days if you took care of my parents."

"Yes. Why?"

"I'm wondering what the ramifications would be if I were unable to stay the whole thirty days?"

He lifted her chin and she looked at his face. "Why?" he asked. "Is something wrong?"

She turned her cheek and his hand fell away. "I'm just really homesick. I don't know if I can make it the whole month."

"Did something happen?"

Tabitha. "No. I've just never been away from my parents this long and it's been harder than I thought."

"I see," he said. But his frown told her he didn't. He placed a hand on her thigh. "I won't force you to stay, Karina. This was never about that."

What was this about, she wanted to ask. But it didn't matter now if he was letting her go.

"What about my parents?" she asked instead. "Will the bank tell them that it was an error?"

He shook his head. "I wouldn't do that to them. Or you."

"Thank you," she whispered. She remembered the dress—the five-thousand-dollar dress—that he had just bought her sight unseen. "I was thinking I could head home Sunday, after the event."

"Are you sure you want to stay until then?"

She nodded "I agreed to it. And besides," she said with a weak smile. "You've bought me a beautiful dress for it. You should at least get to see me in it."

"I can't wait," he said quietly, a sadness in his eyes.

She nodded again and then stood up to leave, but he

grabbed her arm before she walked away.

"What if I arranged for you to go visit?" he pleaded. "Do you think you might want to stay the whole month after all?"

Karina shook her head, not daring to speak. Why was he making this so hard for her?

His grip loosened and she slipped way.

Back in her room, Karina removed the diamond necklace. It was the first time it had come off since Damien had put it on her. She laid it out on the dresser top and pushed it into a perfect circle with her forefinger. She didn't want to accidentally take it home with her.

For the next few days, she and Damien became ships in the night. He had stopped trying and was clearly admitting defeat. And if Karina had thought she was lonely during the days he had been in China, it was worse having him here and all but ignoring her. To sit next to him at dinner and have barely a word pass between them. Every morning he would eat and be gone before she came down.

By Saturday afternoon, Karina had packed her bags and was in the bathroom pinning her thick hair up off her shoulders when there was a knock at the door. She opened it, expecting Damien, but found Romi instead.

"Wow, Miss Watson," she said. "You look amazing."

"Thanks," Karina said, blushing.

"Mr. Bishop said to come downstairs as soon as you're ready. The car is waiting out front."

"Thanks, Romi. Tell him five more minutes."

As Karina grabbed her clutch, she realized that the necklace was no longer on the dresser. Assuming Romi had moved it into a drawer, she made a mental note to ask about it when she got home before heading downstairs.

She felt like a fairy princess as she descended the stairs. The dress moved just as beautifully as it felt, and the hem glided down the steps behind her.

Damien must have heard her footsteps, because he stepped out into the foyer and she was caught off guard by the sight of him in a tuxedo. She was apparently having the same effect on him, because he had stopped in his tracks, and she could see words trying to form on his lips, but no sound came out.

"*¡Ea' Diantre!*" he finally said as she stepped off the bottom stair. "Wow."

"You don't look so bad yourself," she said with the first genuine smile in days.

"You look…stunning."

"I assure you, it's all the dress."

"No," he said, and she was surprised to see the familiar look in his eyes. "It's not. And I think it's missing something." He held out his hand, revealing the missing necklace. "I noticed you hadn't been wearing it and asked Romi to bring it to me if she came across it."

"I didn't want to forget to leave it," she said.

"Wear it one more night."

She turned so that he could put it back on her and again, his hands lingered longer than necessary. She felt his lips softly kiss the nape of her neck and she closed her eyes, relishing the warmth of it.

"Don't go," he whispered so quietly, she wasn't even sure she'd heard him right.

She spun around, stunned.

"Not yet," he said, searching her face.

The door opened and Tom walked in.

"Good, you're both ready," he said. "Shall we head out?"

Karina forced herself to look away. "Lead the way," she said to Tom just as Damien's hand landed on her back, escorting her out to the limousine waiting for them. As she climbed into the back where the two bodyguards were already seated, Damien scooting in next to her, Karina realized she didn't want to go. Not really. Staying longer wouldn't change anything, though.

"So I heard you brought Tabitha to this last year," she said in an effort to remind herself why she was leaving tomorrow.

Tom's head snapped in her direction so fast she was sure he would have whiplash. Damien looked at her in utter confusion.

"Who the hell told you that?" he asked.

"Tabitha herself." She could see Tom's eyes go even wider from the corner of her eye.

"When did you talk to Tabitha?" Damien asked.

"I ran into her at the dress shop," she told him.

Damien laughed, surprising her. "She's jealous."

"Jealous of what? Jealous that you're taking me this year instead of her?"

He laughed even harder, and she heard Tom give a snort.

"Karina, I never took Tabitha to the gala. Or anywhere for that matter."

"But the photo," she said, disgusted that he would so blatantly lie to her. "I saw the photo of you two. The caption even read, 'Tabitha Rose and her date, Damien Bishop.'"

"Yes, we were both there," he said. "And yes, that photo was snapped of us. But she was never my date. We just both happened to be there. When the editor went to publish the picture, he asked for a comment and I had Tom decline for me."

"I did," Tom said, nodding profusely.

"They then asked Tabitha," Damien continued, "who was more than happy to say that I was her date. Even though she was there with someone else—her actual date."

"How did he feel about that?" she asked.

"Who knows," he said, waving a hand. "They were probably broken up by the time the photo was published."

"Why would she do something like that?"

"She's a social climber. She thought my name carried more weight than whoever it was she went with."

Karina sunk into the leather seat, frowning. This changed everything. Or did it? God, she was so confused now.

No one mentioned Tabitha again the rest of the ride, and Tom was excellent at filling the time with small talk. She was understanding more and more why he was in Damien's employment.

When they arrived at the museum hosting the event, everyone piled out of the limo, and Damien was quickly pulled aside for photos in front of a sign bearing the charity and sponsor names. She was surprised when he grabbed her hand, bringing her into the pictures with him.

She did her best to smile pleasantly as he wrapped an arm around her waist. And as the flashes went off, she realized this would be another one for the books. A picture of Damien and a woman who would not appear in any other photos. But as he pulled her tighter into him, causing her to plant a hand on his chest, she wondered if this one would be chaste enough to suggest there was nothing intimate between them.

He kissed the top of her head just before one last flash went off, and then they walked away from the cameras.

"Thank you," he said, leading her into the building.

"I'm surprised you wanted me in the picture," she said. "Considering...."

"I wanted visual proof that I once had you at my side."

"Damien...."

Tom appeared at their side. "I have our table assignments," he said, handing them cards.

Karina found herself cursing Tom yet again.

"And they want you in the back right after dinner," he continued. "They'll introduce you, and then you're on."

"Got it. Tom, will you give Karina and me a moment?" Damien asked.

"Of course, I'll see you two at the table."

Tom walked away and Damien led Karina somewhere less crowded.

"Is Tabitha the reason you want to go home?" he asked.

"It was part of it," she admitted. "But it was more than that."

"What then? Please. Tell me what I can do to make you stay."

"I'm just not sure what I'm doing here."

"I *want* you here."

"Why? What does that even mean?"

He frowned. "To be honest, I'm not sure how to answer that. I just wish you wouldn't leave yet. Weren't we having fun before I left?" He leaned in closer. "What about the boat?"

She smiled. He was right, she had been enjoying herself until Tabitha came along with her toxic words. And if they were both having fun, what was the harm in staying another couple weeks?

She nodded.

"Is that a yes?" he asked, smiling.

"I'll stay the last two weeks." She saw a flash of something in his face, like she'd said something wrong, but it was gone in an instant.

"Thank you," he said, taking her hand and pulling her into him.

She was about to kiss him when they were interrupted again—what was wrong with these people?—this time by someone who just wanted to say hello.

"We should get to our table," Damien said when the man finally left. "I want to eat something before I have to get up and speak."

He took her hand as they walked to the table.

"Does this mean we're still at a stalemate then?" he asked as they approached, and she laughed.

"I'm afraid so."

He kissed her hand, a playful look in his eyes. Little did he know that Karina had every intention of letting him win that night. Tonight she was climbing into whatever bed Damien was in.

They sat at the table where most everyone else, including Tom, was halfway through dinner.

Damien leaned toward Karina.

"Were you actually jealous of Tabitha?" he whispered, laying the cloth napkin on his lap.

"Maybe," she whispered back.

"Well you shouldn't be," he said and started cutting into the steak on his plate. "That woman couldn't hold a candle to you."

"Thank you. How anyone can stand to be around her I'll never know. She's so two-faced."

"Everyone here is," he said quietly with a chuckle. "You shouldn't worry about it. What's the phrase? Don't get your panties in a twist?"

She leaned in even closer until their cheeks were, almost touching and whispered, "Well you don't have to worry about that because I'm not wearing any."

Damien stopped cutting his steak, his grip tightening around the silverware until his knuckles were almost white.

"You're joking, right?" he whispered.

"Nope," she said with a smile. "I didn't have any that wouldn't leave an obvious panty-line, so I—"

He slammed his knife and fork down, causing some of the other diners to look at him.

"Will you excuse us?" he said, standing abruptly.

He took her arm and pulled her up with him. The

movements were gentle, but his grip was strong.

"Where are we going?" she asked as he led her out of the dining area.

"You win," was all he said.

The Victor

"I WIN?" KARINA repeated as Damien pulled her along an empty hall. "What does that—oh god! But what about your speech?"

"This won't take long," he said breathlessly. He opened a door marked "supplies" and shoved her into the tiny room before closing the door behind him.

His mouth was instantly on hers, and she wrapped her arms around his neck as she fell against a shelf. He turned so that her back was on the door and he hitched the dress up to her waist where, true to her word, she had no underwear.

"God, there's so many things I want to do to you right now," he said, pressing his forehead to hers, the pair of them drawing heavy breaths.

"You talk too much," she said, undoing his pants. "Shut up and fuck me already."

"With pleasure," he growled as he cupped her ass

beneath the dress, and she gave a sharp little cry as he thrust into her.

She wrapped her arms back around him as he did it again, and this time she bit her lip. And again, and again, and Karina was in ecstasy. Damien's breath was hot against her neck as he continued to drive into her, filling her, and it wasn't long before she could feel the orgasm building and then her fingers pulled at the hair at his nape as the fire exploded inside her—it was all she could do not to scream out. Just as it was about to ebb, he moved faster, prolonging the climax, and with one last movement, his body went still against hers.

Karina rested her head against the wall behind her, trying to catch her breath. "I win," she gasped out, staring at the ceiling as the last currents of electricity faded from her body.

Damien gave a chuckle, and she met his eyes.

"Yes, you do," he said before kissing her hard and passionately. "Wait until we get home. Then I'll show you what it really means to be the victor."

"I can't wait," she said with a big grin.

"We should probably get back out there," he said.

"You're supposed to be giving a speech soon."

He carefully stepped back and turned around to fix his pants while she adjusted the gown's skirt around her, wishing she had worn underwear after all. She had a feeling she might be ruining another dress. This time was worth it though.

Damien opened the door, and after checking that the coast was clear, they both stepped out into the hall.

"Hold on," she said and started fixing his hair, flattening the back where she had messed it up. "How do I look?" she asked when she had finished.

"Radiant," he said with a smile.

"You know what I mean," she said, giving him a

playful push.

"Turn around," he said and she did. She could feel him struggling to put a pin back in when someone shouted at them.

"There you two are!"

They both looked to see Tom rushing down the hall in a panic.

"They're waiting for you!" he said. "That's your introduction they're giving up there right now!"

"Wish me luck," Damien said, and he blew her a kiss as he ran off.

Tom stood there looking curiously at Damien's disappearing figure, then to Karina.

"You guys didn't—did you just…." He threw both hands up as he turned away. "You know what, I don't even want to know."

Karina felt her cheeks turning bright red but said nothing and followed Tom back out to their table. She sat down at her seat just as Damien walked out onto the stage.

She loved hearing his voice fill the room, and he did a wonderful job of looking out at the audience, at everyone but her. And then about five minutes into it, he locked eyes with her and it was obvious that he had lost his train of thought. He tried to cover it up by taking a sip from the glass of water on the podium, and she forced herself to look down so that he could finish.

"This is your doing," Tom whispered, leaning across Damien's empty seat so only she could hear.

Karina's blush deepened as she remained silent, continuing to look down at her hands while a slow smile spread across her face.

After his speech, Damien insisted they head home even though there was another hour left to the event. Karina had no complaints. All she cared about was getting home and holding him to his word. Yet as they tried to make their way to the entrance, people kept stopping them to chat with Damien. As always, he was polite and gracious, though he never let go of Karina's hand. As if he feared she would disappear into the crowd if he loosened his grip on her.

Finally they were all climbing back into the limousine. It seemed like forever until it was just her and Damien in the house, and she was positively buzzing as he secured the front door. The quickie at the museum had only whet her appetite for this man.

The security panel beeped, signaling everything was locked up for the night, and he turned to face her, the intense look in his eyes.

"You look lovely in that dress," he said, still holding the jacket he had removed on the drive home.

"Thank you," she replied.

"And I can't wait to get you out of it."

"The zipper's right here," she said, reaching around to her back, but he stopped her.

"Wait," he said. "There's too many windows. I don't need my men accidentally seeing what I'm about to do to you."

Her pulse quickened. "To your room then," she whispered.

"I was beginning to think I'd never hear you say those words," he said as he took her hand and pulled her up the stairs with him.

They walked into the room and Damien closed the door, locking it. He tossed the jacket on a nearby chair and pulled off the loosened bow tie while she kicked her heels off in the same general direction, giggling. She reached around again for the zipper of the dress.

"Allow me," he said, and she turned her back to him.

With one palm on her bare skin, he slowly unzipped the dress with his other hand. The gown cascaded down around her to the floor, leaving her completely naked in the middle of his bedroom.

"You mean to tell me," he said, kissing her shoulder, "that this single article of clothing was the only thing between me and your exquisite body this whole evening?"

She trembled as he kneeled down behind her, his lips leaving a hot trail down her back while his hands glided down her thighs. "That and the tux you're still wearing," she said, struggling to get the words out.

"I'll take care of that eventually," he said. "I want to torture you a while longer."

"And how do you plan to do that?" she asked breathlessly as he stood up again, and she turned to face him.

"By taking my sweet time with you," he said before kissing her.

As their tongues danced, Karina worked at the buttons of his shirt. Why did there have to be so many of them? Damien came to her assistance by simply ripping the last of them open, and after she helped push it off of him, he wrapped his arms around her. His chest was hot and hard against hers and it wasn't enough. She wedged her hands between them, trying to get at his zipper, but he stopped her by picking her up until she wrapped her legs around his waist. Nice to know his muscles weren't just for show. Keeping one arm wrapped around her, he managed to pull the covers back with one hand before dropping her onto the bed. He kicked off his shoes and socks as quickly as possible and then climbed on the bed, still wearing his pants.

"You forgot something," she said, trying to work at his pants again when he straddled her, placing his hands on either side of her.

"I told you," he said, kissing her neck while moving his waist down away from her reach. "There'll be plenty of time for that later."

She groaned as his kisses moved down to her chest. And then she closed her eyes, running her hands through his soft hair as he sucked on one breast, then the other. His mouth didn't stay at it for long before continuing its path south, and Karina spread her legs, knowing exactly what he planned to do.

"Oh," she moaned as his fingers opened her up, allowing easier access for his tongue. The pleasure of it made her delirious, and she found herself pushing harder against his mouth.

"Don't stop," she whispered, and he responded by licking and sucking even harder until—for the second time that night—she was coming for him.

To her disappointment, he stopped, cutting her orgasm short.

She propped herself up on her elbows as he slid off the end of the bed, and she watched him remove his pants with difficulty due to the erection burdening him.

"Does this mean you're done torturing me?" she asked.

"Not quite," he said with a grin. "Roll over."

She did gladly, eager to see what else he had in store for her. With her cheek on the pillow, she waited until she felt his mouth on her calf. Slowly he worked his way up her legs, a kiss here, a nip there, until he reached her ass, where he sank his teeth a little harder, just enough to make her moan. His lips grazed her back up to her neck and she felt the weight of him on top of her, felt his erection against her. One of his hands slipped under her hips until his fingers found just what they were searching for as he buried his mouth into her neck.

"God you taste good," he said into her ear and she tried twisting beneath him, unable to take it anymore. She wanted Damien in her again

He moved off of her and she rolled onto her side so that

she could face him, bringing her mouth to his. As her tongue slipped past his lips, he cupped her face with one hand and she pushed him onto his back, throwing her leg over his waist. She slid down onto him, and both his hands moved to her hips, where she could feel his fingers pressing tightly into her flesh. It wasn't long before she felt another orgasm building within her and she sat up, digging her nails into his chest. She rocked harder against him and felt the fire ignite in her belly, extending all the way to her toes, her fingers, even her cheeks, as she arched her back. Damien kept his grip on her hips, kept her moving, and she thought it would never end. She didn't want it to end. But it did, and as it faded away, she slowed down, trying to catch her breath.

She leaned forward and kissed him.

"You're not done already, are you?" he asked.

"Not even close," she purred.

As she sat up and rocked against him again, she knew she was already close. What was it about him that elicited the fire from her so quickly? Each one came quicker than the last and still she wanted just one more—each time, Damien obliged until she barely had the energy to move with him. He rolled her easily onto her back, taking advantage of the spacious bed, and she wrapped her legs around his waist as he quickly moved in and out of her, finally succumbing to his own climax.

She looked up into his eyes as he breathed heavily above her, a light sheen on his face. He shook his head slightly.

"What?" she asked with a frown.

"Just thinking how beautiful you look right now," he said with a grin.

"I can only imagine what a hot mess I must look like right now."

"You're right about the hot part," he said and she

laughed.

He kissed her before rolling back onto the bed and Karina slid out of it, intending to head back to her room to rinse off some of the sweat.

"Where are you going?" he asked, reaching across the bed for her.

"To my room. I need a shower."

"Use mine."

"Are you going to join me?" she asked.

"I'm not sure if I can stand on my own two feet right now."

"Well you'll know where to find me," she said, walking into his bathroom and leaving the door open.

"Give me a minute to gather my strength," he sighed.

Karina turned on the water, giggling. She loved the idea of wearing him out. The water warmed quickly and she stepped in, expecting Damien to be right behind her. When she finally realized he wasn't coming, she turned off the water and grabbed a towel. She walked back into the room to find Damien in exactly the same position she had left him in. Realizing now that she really had exhausted him, she pulled the twisted comforter up over him as best she could and kissed his cheek before returning to her room.

Change of Plans

WHEN KARINA CAME down the next morning, she was surprised to see Damien's place setting still untouched—she had beaten him down to breakfast. Not by much, though, because he came striding in only a couple minutes behind her.

"Good morning," he drawled as he sat down.

"Good morning," she said with a smile. "How'd you sleep?"

"Like a rock. I can't believe I fell asleep on you last night. I had every—"

Romi walked in, cutting him off. No one said anything as she brought out the jug of fresh orange juice.

"Thank you, Romi," he said before she walked away. "I had every intention of joining you in the shower," he whispered when she left the room again. "I closed my eyes for a second and next thing I knew, it was morning and you were gone."

"I suppose you'll just have to make it up to me then," she said, leaning in close to him.

"What did you have in mind?"

"Hmm…" Karina gazed out the window behind Damien and saw the open water. "What if you take me out on the boat again?"

The corner of his mouth went up, revealing a dimple. "That sounds like a great idea." He looked at his watch. "We just have to be back by four," he said with a frown.

"Why is that?"

"I'm flying up to New York tonight."

Now she frowned. "Why?"

"I have a meeting tomorrow. It's easier if I fly up the night before. I'll be back tomorrow night."

"Will you do me a favor?" she asked.

"Anything," he said.

"Will you have Tom give me a copy of your itinerary for the next two weeks?"

There was a flash of something in his face again, the same as last night.

"Because it's getting real annoying not knowing if you're coming or going," she continued, ignoring it.

"Absolutely," he said. To her surprise, he pulled out his phone and started tapping away. "Done," he said, setting it aside. "I'm sure he'll have it to you before we leave. Now what do you say we get going on this boat trip so we have time for…other things?"

She leaned toward him again. "I couldn't agree more."

He held her face with one hand and kissed her, making her almost forget they were still sitting at the breakfast table.

"You go change," he whispered, finally pulling away. "And meet me at the boat."

Less than ten minutes later, Karina was boarding the

boat, wearing smarter shoes that she had found among the closet's collection.

"You remembered," Damien said as he glanced down at her feet.

"I'm a quick study," she said.

"Does that mean I can let you sail for us today?"

She grimaced. "Okay, maybe not that quick."

Once again Damien let her take the helm, and even though she would have been fine on her own, he remained behind her and she preferred it that way. This time, they stayed closer to the Miami shore, and he pointed landmarks out to her. Eventually they anchored, but instead of bringing a picnic basket up top, he led her to the berth below.

"I was going to sleep with you the last time we were on this boat," Karina said afterward as her naked body lay across Damien's, her chin on his chest.

"I don't believe you," he said and she laughed.

"It's true."

"Damn Tom."

"That's what I said."

Karina turned her head so that her cheek was now flat against his chest, and he started caressing her back. Between the gently rocking ship and the steady beat of his heart, she was sure she'd fall asleep.

"You should set an alarm," she murmured. "Just in case we both doze off. Wouldn't want you to miss New York."

"I was thinking about that. New York I mean. I think you should come with me."

She repositioned herself so she could look at him. "Really? Aren't you just going to be in meetings the whole time? What would I do?"

"It's New York," he said. "There's plenty to do. My hotel is right next to Central Park—"

"Of course it is."

"—so you'd be able to wander wherever your heart desires."

"Maybe…"

"Have you been to New York before?"

"I went once for a concert when I was a freshman in college. We only spent the night, though."

"You should definitely come with me. You deserve to see more of it."

"But aren't you only spending the one night?"

"Only for you," he said. "If you came with, I could extend it a day or two."

Only for you. The words made her heart race, and she hoped Damien couldn't feel it. He didn't want her to be bored. Surely that's all he meant by it.

"I think," she said, tracing her finger in a figure-eight pattern on his chest, "you just want me there to keep your bed warm."

"That would be a bonus, I suppose," he said with a wicked smile. "Does this mean you'll come?"

"Oh, I'll come," she said, sliding a leg over his hips until she was straddling him. Leaning forward, she gave him a quick kiss before moving to nip at his ear. "I will definitely…come," she whispered.

It was with reluctance that they headed up top and made the journey back to the house. This time Karina wasn't dreading it so much, since she no longer had to say goodbye to Damien. At least not tonight. As the house came into view, she was painfully aware that they had exactly two weeks and one day until she went home. She pushed the thought to the back of her mind, determined to enjoy every last second with him.

"You should visit your parents while we're up there," Damien said as they climbed off the boat.

She frowned. "You do realize that my parents don't live

in New York, right?"

"Of course I do. But I could get you a train ticket. It's only a couple hours' ride, isn't it?"

"It's a nice thought, but how am I supposed to explain why I'm popping in for the day if they think I'm in Miami?"

"I don't get it," Damien said with a tilt of his head. "Tell them you're in New York City for a couple days and wanted to say hi."

"But how do I explain what I'm doing in New York?"

Damien grabbed her arm, pausing her. "What exactly do your parents think you're doing down here?"

"I told them I was down here for work, that I'm helping to open another store. What was I supposed to tell them?"

"The truth?"

She laughed harshly. "You're joking."

"Do they know *anything* about me?"

She shook her head. "Why would they?"

"Where do they think the money came from?" he asked, frowning.

"I don't know. But they have no idea it has anything to do with me."

"You mean they seriously aren't questioning it?"

"My mom wants to believe it's a miracle," she said. "Knowing my dad, he's probably poking around. Don't be surprised if you get a fruit basket delivered one day."

"Why wouldn't you tell them about where you were going? About me?"

"Because they never would have let me do this. They would've freaked at the thought of me going to spend a month with some guy I don't even know, let alone because he paid all their bills. You must realize how this looks."

"Yet you came," he said, his expression softening. "You didn't tell them so you could come."

"I came because you kept your end of the deal. The

truth is…" She remembered how she had planned to tell him the deal was off.

"The truth is what?" he asked.

"It's nothing."

"The truth is what, Karina?"

"There you two are," Tom called out, and they both looked up to see him coming out onto the lawn. For once, Karina was glad for his intrusion.

"You're early," Damien said, frowning.

"I'm always early," Tom said, looking puzzled. "I brought the itinerary you asked for. It's on the kitchen counter."

"There's been a change of plans for tonight," Damien told him. "Karina's coming with us."

"Oh," Tom said with raised eyebrows.

"I hope that's okay," Karina said.

"He's the boss," Tom answered. It didn't exactly make Karina feel any better.

"And we'll be staying an extra night or two if nothing comes up," said Damien.

"Of course." Tom turned to Karina. "Do you need any help with packing?"

"No, thank you. I think I've got it," she said as the three of them headed back into the house. "Is there anything special I should bring, though?"

"I'd recommend a good dress for dinner," Damien told her. "Other than that, bring whatever you feel comfortable in."

"Got it. I'll go get ready then."

As she left them in the kitchen, she couldn't shake the feeling that they were waiting for her to leave before talking, and she paused around the corner.

"What is it?" she heard Damien ask.

"I'm just surprised you're bringing her along," Tom replied.

"She's my guest," said Damien. "I can't keep abandoning her."

"Ah, is that what it is?" Tom asked, and Karina rushed off to her room before she could hear anything else.

She was right, Damien just felt bad about her being bored.

Late that night, they were walking into Damien's suite while Tom and the bodyguards retreated to their own rooms nearby.

"You mean I don't get my own room?"

"I didn't realize you would want your own room. Is it a problem?"

"I'm sure I could make do," she said, wrapping her arms around his neck.

"Are you sure?" he said, pulling her hips into him. "Because I could easily arrange for you to have your own suite."

"Then I'd just have to do the walk of shame to it later tonight."

"So you're willing to stay here with me out of convenience?"

"Only if you make it worth my while," she said with a smile.

"Then I guess I'd better get started." He picked her up and she giggled as he carried her into the bedroom.

Karina lay awake in bed while Damien slept soundly next to her, his arm across her chest. Too many thoughts were racing through her head, making it impossible to fall asleep. And they all centered around Damien.

It was all his fault. She could be home now, asleep in her own bed, probably tired from another long day at the coffee shop. Now she wondered how she was supposed to go back to that life two weeks from now. How was she supposed to forget what Damien was doing to her, what he was causing her to feel?

Deciding she needed some distance from him, she carefully slipped out from under his arm and put on the nearest article of clothing—Damien's dress shirt on the floor by the bed.

It smelled like him, but at least it wasn't warm or breathing softly against her neck.

She moved out to the living room and stood in front of the window facing Central Park. People were still milling along the sidewalks, even at this hour, but there was little movement in the park—just a maze of lights from the street lamps lining the paths.

A chill swept over her and she stepped over to the couch, where she wrapped the throw blanket around her shoulders before sitting on it, tucking her feet beneath her. She laid her head on the armrest, her eyelids finally feeling heavy, and wondered if she had been right about there being no harm in staying until the end of the month.

"Karina?"

She opened her eyes to see Damien crouched down next to her, worry all over his face.

"Is everything okay?" he asked as she realized she was still on the couch and light was streaming in through the window.

"Yeah," she said, sitting up. "I was having trouble sleeping and came out here. I didn't mean to spend the whole night here."

"You'd tell me if something was wrong, wouldn't you?"

"Of course," she lied. "Do you have to leave?"

"Soon," he said. "Do you have any idea what you want to do today?"

"I'm not sure. Maybe visit some museums."

Damien stood up and pulled the wallet from his back pocket.

"This should get you through the day," he said, handing her several hundred-dollar bills.

Karina looked at them, wanting to say no. The problem was that she didn't actually have any cash of her own at the moment.

"It's okay," he said with a chuckle. "They won't bite."

"I just feel bad accepting it," she said.

"Don't. I invited you up here, and I want you to enjoy yourself. I promised I would take care of everything for you when you agreed to come to Miami with me."

"I know. It's just that—"

There was a knock at the door.

"That must be Tom," said Damien.

"I should go hide in the bedroom," Karina said, standing. "He probably doesn't need to see me in nothing but your shirt."

"Don't worry," he said with a small smile. "Tom's gay, so it won't affect him the way it's affecting me right now."

She wrapped her arms around him. "It's a shame you have to go," she said just as Tom knocked again.

"If I came back and you were still wearing only that, I wouldn't complain one bit."

"Go," she said and kissed him before heading to the bedroom.

"I'm leaving the money here on the table," he called out. "Use it."

The door shut behind him and Karina climbed into the shower, excited to explore Manhattan.

Karina was immediately glad she had agreed to come with Damien. Even though he was going to be in meetings all day, it was so much easier to get out and about on her own without relying on Damien's staff.

After spending the day exploring the Metropolitan Museum of Art and the Guggenheim, she made it back to the room only a half hour before Damien.

"I don't know about you, but I'm starving," he said as he loosened his tie. "You ready to head out for dinner?"

"Are you kidding?" she called from the couch where she was sprawled. "I've just spent all day walking around. I need to rest my feet."

"We'll eat here in the hotel. They have a great bistro downstairs."

"Will it require me to wear heels?"

"Well, I wouldn't recommend wearing sneakers," he said as he sat on the edge of the couch.

She sighed. "I don't think I could squeeze my poor feet into anything tight even if I wanted to. Which I don't."

He kissed her forehead. "I'm sure any flats you have will be fine."

"Thank you."

Ten minutes later, Damien had lost the tie completely and swapped his suit jacket for a sports coat. Karina came out of the bedroom in black flats and the same wrap dress she had worn to the engagement party and watched as Damien shook his head, smiling.

"You do remember what I said about this dress, don't you?" he asked, fingering the bow tied at her waist.

"How could I forget?"

He gave a gentle tug, not enough to loosen it. "I'm not sure we'll make it down to dinner."

"I thought you were starving. So much so that you couldn't let my poor little feet take a rest."

"I've changed my mind," he murmured into her ear.

"Too bad," she said, pushing him away and walking over to her purse. "I've gotten dressed up for you. Now you're taking me to dinner."

"Fair enough. But you might have to make it up to me

later."

"Gladly," she said with a wicked smile.

There was already a small crowd at the hostess booth, and Karina watched as Damien shook hands with the maître d', who left to go check on their table.

"I could always tell him to just put our name down for twenty minutes later," he whispered as they waited.

She fiddled with the lapel of his jacket. "You really think twenty minutes would be long enough?"

"Probably not," he said and kissed her right there in front of everyone.

Her phone started ringing and she reluctantly pulled away, digging it out of her purse to see that it was her mom.

"Hey, Mom," she said, shooting Damien a glance just as the maître d' returned. "What's up?" she asked.

"Karina, sweetie, are you in New York City by any chance?" her mom asked.

"Why would you think that?" Karina asked, her heart beating fast.

"It's just that I'm sitting in a restaurant and I swear I saw you kissing some guy in the lobby."

Karina stopped in the middle of the dining room and did a mad spin, looking. It couldn't be.

"Oh my god!" her mother squealed into the phone. "It *is* you!"

And then Karina saw her. The woman waving madly from her seat in the far corner as she hung up the phone

"What is it?" Damien said.

"Oh god," said Karina as she watched her mother and father sitting patiently at the table, waiting for her to go over to them.

"What's going on?" asked Damien, putting a hand on her arm.

"Get ready to meet my parents."

Confusion

"YOUR PARENTS ARE *here*?" Damien asked.

Karina pointed to where they were sitting, watching, still waiting.

"What are they doing here?"

"I have no idea," she said as she started walking their way.

"Will you excuse us a minute?" she heard Damien say to the maître d'. "We've just seen someone we know."

"Of course, sir."

Karina's mother stood as she and Damien neared the table.

"I can't believe it's you," her mother said, giving her a quick hug before holding her at arm's length. "Wow, Karina, you look so good! You look *tan*. What are you doing in Manhattan?"

"I'm visiting for a couple days," she said, risking a quick glance at Damien. "What are *you* guys doing here?"

"We realized we hadn't been able to get away in a while," her mother said, sitting back down in her chair. "Not since…. Well, since we weren't feeling so strapped this month, we thought we'd spend the weekend in New York. We catch the train home tomorrow."

"Are you staying here at the hotel?" Karina asked.

"Oh lord no! We aren't feeling *that* well off. We just came for—"

"Who's your friend?" her father asked, speaking for the first time.

"Mom, Dad," she said, looking nervously at both of them. "This is Damien Bishop. Damien, these are my parents, Cheri and Ron."

Damien extended his hand first to Cheri, who accepted it, then to Ron, who wouldn't budge.

"It's a pleasure to meet you both," Damien said, sliding the rejected hand into his trouser pocket.

"I didn't know you were dating anyone," Cheri said, giving Karina a playful swat on the arm. "How did you two meet? Do you live here in the city?"

"Damien lives in Miami, Mom. I met him when he came into the coffee shop." Technically every word of it was true.

"I had to come up here for business," Damien explained, "and I invited Karina to join me."

"How exciting!" her mother gushed.

Karina noticed her dad was awfully silent, refusing to even smile. She wanted to believe it was the thought of his little girl going away with a man he'd never met that had him so quiet, but she suspected it was more than that. And it worried her.

"We should probably let you guys get back to your meal," said Karina. "We have a table waiting for us—"

"Nonsense," said her mother. "There's plenty of room at our table, and we haven't even ordered yet. You don't mind, Ron, do you?"

Ron gave a grunt.

"Really, we wouldn't want to intrude," Karina said.

"Please," Cheri begged, her eyes wide. "Have dinner with us. We miss you."

Karina looked to Damien for help.

"It's okay," he said quietly, not understanding that this was the last thing she wanted. "Really. I'll go tell the maître d' we won't need our table after all and have him grab a couple chairs."

"That's so sweet," said Cheri.

Karina had never felt so awkward around her parents as Damien rushed off.

"That dress is adorable, sweetie," her mom said. "Where did you find it?"

Karina looked down at the designer dress. "Um, would you believe at Goodwill?" Again, not really a lie, since she was simply asking a question.

"Get out of here! Why can't I ever find gems like that at the thrift stores? And it fits you so perfectly."

"Just lucky, I guess."

Fortunately Damien wasn't long, and a waiter was right behind him bringing two extra chairs. Cheri slid her chair over to sit next to Ron, and Karina sat down between Damien and her father. The last two men in the world she wanted in a room together. The man who had raised her to be a strong, independent woman, and the man who had essentially bought her.

"So Damien, what exactly is it that you do?" Cheri asked.

Damien cleared his throat as Karina held her breath.

"I'm in software development and sales," he said, and she allowed herself to exhale.

"And do you get to travel a lot for work?" Cheri asked.

"I do," Damien answered.

A server arrived just then and took everyone's order.

"So sweetie," Cheri said with a smile when that was all done. "Why didn't you tell us you were seeing someone?"

Karina could feel herself turn beet red, as well as Damien giving her knee a squeeze under the table.

"Well," she said, blushing as she looked at Damien. "It's still new."

"Yet you know him well enough to come all the way to New York with him," her father said.

"Oh, Ron. You hush," said Cheri.

"I'm just sayin'." Ron muttered.

"Look at Karina," said Cheri. "She's obviously happy. You let her be."

Karina was starting to sweat now. This had been a bad idea. A very bad idea.

"I understand your concerns," Damien said, and Karina prayed for a hole to swallow her up. "But I assure you I have nothing but the best of intentions for your daughter."

Karina snapped her head in his direction. Now that was a blatant lie.

"Could we please not do this?" Karina pleaded, her face reddening even more.

"Please, Ron," Cheri said, placing a hand on his arm.

Ron sighed but said nothing else—until they were halfway through the main course. The conversation had managed to steer toward how work was going for Karina—more lies—and some of the places Damien had visited. Then after a couple glasses of wine, Cheri started talking about their recent "miracle."

"Interesting thing about that, though," Ron said, and Karina closed her eyes, knowing exactly where this was going. "I did a little digging and it turns out that everything had been taken care of by a single, generous man." Karina opened her eyes. "A man by the name of Damien Bishop."

Damien gently set his fork down and pulled the napkin

from his lap, wiping the corner of his mouth with it before placing it next to his plate.

"You never told me that," said Cheri, her eyes wide as she looked from Ron to Damien.

"That's because I was still trying to put all the pieces together," said Ron. "And now I find him here, in New York City, with my one and only daughter."

"Mr. Watson—"

"Is my daughter your whore, Mr. Bishop?" Ron asked, narrowing his eyes at Damien.

"Daddy!"

Ron looked at Karina, and she had never seen him look so sad. Not even when her mom had been diagnosed. "I thought I raised you better than that," he whispered, slowly shaking his head.

"It's not like that," Karina said, her throat burning because that was the biggest lie of them all. Sort of.

Ron stood and started pulling dollar bills from his wallet.

"I've got this, sir," Damien said. "Don't worry about it."

"I won't have my daughter pay for it later," Ron snapped.

Damien stood as well. "I've never treated Karina with anything but respect," he said, his voice stern.

"Let's go, Cheri," said Ron. "I've lost my appetite."

They all looked at Karina's mom, who was sitting there dumbfounded, still trying to register everything that was happening.

"Is this all true?" she asked from across the table.

"No," Karina said, shaking her head.

"Then what is it, sweetie?"

Karina's face fell, and she fought back the tears. There was no better explanation to give.

"We're leaving," Ron said as Cheri finally got up from

her chair. He held his hand out. "You can come with us, Karina."

She looked from her father to Damien, then back to Ron. "I—I don't want to."

Ron sighed and started to pull her mother with him toward the exit, but Cheri stopped and walked around the table to Karina, pressing a hand to her cheek.

"I love you, honey," she said. "You call if you need anything."

"It's not like that," Karina whispered again as her mother and father walked away.

Damien placed a hand on her shoulder as he called a waiter over.

"We need the check, please," she heard him say, and then he was helping her out of the chair.

They made it as far as the elevator before she was burying her face into his chest and letting the tears finally fall.

"I'm so sorry," he whispered as he wrapped his arms around her.

"Do you understand now?" she asked, looking up at him. "Do you understand why I didn't want to tell them the truth?"

"I had no idea," he said as he wiped her cheek with his thumb. "It's not true though. You and I both know it's not true."

Karina rested her head against his chest again as the elevator continued its ascent.

"Isn't it though?" she asked. "Wasn't this all about getting me into your bed?"

"Yes…and no." Damien lifted her chin with his finger. "I think we both know it's not as simple as that," he said before kissing her.

He was right, it wasn't as simple as that. But Karina wasn't sure she understood exactly what it was just yet.

The elevator doors opened and their lips parted.

"I wish I'd never come here," she said as they approached the door to their room. "New York has been ruined for me."

"You can't mean that," he said, unlocking the door and letting her in first.

"You realize my father called me a whore."

"He's just confused by the whole thing."

"You know what, Damien," she said, spinning around to face him. "So am I. Tell me what about this doesn't make me one. The money may not have gone directly to me, but you sure paid a pretty penny for me to be here."

She crossed her arms, and Damien rested his hands on her shoulders.

"That night I came to see you at work," he said, "you told me that you had too much on your plate to even consider my offer. I was simply giving you the freedom to say yes."

"Freedom? Don't you mean you twisted my arm?"

He scowled at her, removing his hands to plant them on his waist. "Is that what you think?" he said. "I gave you the choice. You could've said no. But you said yes, Karina." He swallowed hard. "You said yes."

"Because I didn't think you were serious," she said quietly. "I had no idea you were in any position to make it happen."

The pained expression on Damien's face shocked her.

"I was planning to tell you that I had changed my mind," she explained. "And then my mom called and it turned out you had already taken care of everything."

He gripped the back of a nearby chair, leaning against it. It was obvious that he was hurting, and it confused Karina. Why did it hurt him to hear this if he'd only been trying to sleep with her? And why was her heart aching to see him this way?

He looked up at her and she stood there, wringing her hands, fearing what he would say next.

"Do you regret coming to Miami with me?" he asked.

"No," she whispered, shaking her head. "I don't."

Damien stood and pulled the phone from his pocket.

"Who are you calling?" she asked.

He turned away from her before speaking into the phone. "Tom. I need you to call Jim and tell him to get the plane ready. We're heading home tonight after all."

"We're leaving?" she said when he hung up.

"I think we're both done with New York," he said as he walked into the bedroom, presumably to pack, and she followed him to where he stopped at the end of the bed, his back to her.

"I say something you don't want to hear," she said, "and now you're ready to run back home?"

He turned to face her.

"You just said New York was ruined for you. Are you telling me you'd rather stay?"

"What does it matter if I was going to change my mind?' she asked.

"You're right," he sighed. "It's doesn't matter."

She took a step forward and pushed him until he fell back onto the bed before climbing on top of him.

"What the hell are you doing?" he asked.

"Isn't this what you want?" she asked, undoing his belt. "Isn't this why you brought me along on your business trip?"

"Stop it, Karina!" he shouted, fighting off her hands as he sat up, causing her to fall onto the floor with a thud. "I'm so sorry!" he said, jumping off the bed to help her up.

"What's the problem?" she asked, wrenching her hand away when she was back on two feet. She looked him square in the eye, her blood coursing hotly through her. "You don't want me anymore?"

"What? That's ridiculous."

"Then fuck me, Damien," she said, and he frowned, running a hand through his hair as she pulled on the tie holding her dress together. "Fuck me like you meant it."

There was a pause, and she watched a darkness cloud his expression before he suddenly slipped a hand beneath her dress, slamming her hips into him.

"Be careful what you ask for," he growled, placing his other hand at the base of her neck where he grabbed a fistful of hair, forcing her lips up to his.

The kiss was angry and primal, and she welcomed it as she pressed her hands to his chest. This she could understand. At least for this moment, there was no confusion about what he wanted from her.

He forced her back against the wall and roughly ran his hand down between her legs. She groaned at his touch and pulled the dress shirt from his waistband before ripping it open, causing buttons to fall silently onto the carpet at their feet.

He pulled away, scowling at her, but said nothing as the hand in her hair yanked again, lifting her chin to expose her neck, and she closed her eyes as he buried his mouth into it. She dug her nails into his chest, and the hand between her thighs left briefly as Damien undid his own pants before returning, simply sliding her underwear to the side to give him access. She wrapped her right leg around him and he plunged into her, deep and hard, her shoulder blades slamming against the wall with the force of it.

"Is this what you wanted?" he asked, releasing her hair to hold the leg around him.

"Yes!" she screamed as he drove into her again. "God, yes," she panted, and he kissed her as he gripped her other leg, lifting her off the floor completely. Still locked together at the hips, he walked backwards until he hit the edge of the bed and fell back onto it, Karina on top of him.

He tried to sit up, to face her, but she pushed him back down on the bed, sinking her nails even deeper into his chest until he grimaced from the pain of it.

"Is this what *you* wanted, Mr. Bishop?" she asked and saw a flash of anger in his eyes before he gripped her ass so tightly she was sure she would bruise from the pressure. It only made her grind that much harder against him, and before she knew it, she was climaxing with Damien growling only seconds later as he released everything he had into her.

Karina fell forward, planting her hands on either side of his head, feeling more exhausted than the brief minutes should have warranted, and found herself unable to look him in the eye. She focused instead on his chest, still rising rapidly as he struggled to catch his breath, red marks visible from where she had clawed him.

"I hope you're getting your money's worth," she muttered as she climbed off and wrapped her dress back around her.

Damien said nothing, and she forced herself to glance at him. The tormented look on his face only made her stomach knot. Slightly ashamed of herself, she walked to the bathroom and locked the door behind her. She sat on the edge of the tub, wanting to cry at her childish behavior. But no tears came.

Two hours later, the five of them were boarding the plane, Jim and his co-pilot already in the cockpit. Damien sat down across from her, though he had said very little since she'd left him on the bed. Even now, he rested his chin in his palm and looked out the window.

"Do you guys want anything before we take off?" Tom asked.

"We're fine," Damien said, looking up at him. "We won't be needing anything. Just sit down and relax." He went back to gazing out the dark window.

Karina watched Tom look from Damien to her, puzzled. She averted her eyes, and he walked away without saying anything else.

"I'm sorry," she whispered.

He didn't look up, and she wasn't sure if he'd heard her.

"It's not your fault," he finally whispered back.

The plane started moving, and Karina braced herself for the longest four hours of her life.

The Fall

IT WAS LONG past midnight by the time Damien and Karina walked into the house. To her surprise, he took her hand as they walked up the stairs—a good sign, she decided. When they reached her door, however, she stopped and pulled her hand from his before he could continue to his own room.

"Is everything okay?" he asked, facing her.

"I'm going to turn in for the night," she said.

He frowned. "In your room?"

"It's late and I'm exhausted, and I'm sure you are too."

"I see."

"I'll see you in the morning though, right?"

He closed the short distance between them and took her face in both his hands before kissing her. It was slow and sensual and awakened so much in her, but Karina didn't know if she had the energy to be in his bed tonight.

"This was never about buying you," he said. "I hope

you know that."

"Then what was it about?" she asked desperately.

He scowled. "I—I don't know. I don't know how to explain it."

She sighed. "Good night, Damien."

"Are you sure?" he asked.

She nodded. "I think it's for the best," she whispered. "At least for tonight."

He kissed her forehead and walked away.

Karina changed into leggings and a tank top before crawling into bed, her lips still swollen from his kiss. As she lay there, waiting for sleep to comfort her, she found herself remembering every word Damien had said to her in the hotel room. And she wondered why the more he said to her, the more confused she became.

Karina wasn't all that surprised when she came downstairs the next morning to find that Damien had gone into the office. He turned up just as Romi was setting the table for dinner. The timing was so perfect that Karina knew he must have given her a heads-up.

"How was your day?" he asked politely as he spooned some vegetables onto his plate.

"I missed you," she said and watched his hand stop in mid-air for a split second.

"I thought you needed some time to yourself," he said, continuing what he was doing without looking at her.

She placed a hand on his arm, and he finally met her eye.

"Do you still want me here?" she asked.

"Of course."

"Then why are you avoiding me?"

"I told you, I thought you needed some space."

She shook her head. "I don't have much time left here," she said. "I want to spend it with you."

He picked up her hand and kissed the palm of it. "I agree," he said.

Darkness had completely fallen by the time they finished dinner, and Damien grabbed the open bottle of wine and their glasses from the table before leading Karina outside.

"Where are we going?" she asked.

"To gaze at the stars," he said with a coy smile.

She followed him to the end of the dock, where he removed his shoes and rolled up his pants. She did the same, and soon they were sitting side by side with their toes in the water.

"Should I worry about sharks eating my feet?" she asked as he filled their wine glasses.

"So long as you're not bleeding into the water, you should be fine."

"Not exactly reassuring."

He handed her the glass. "What are your plans when you go home?" he asked.

"Go back to school, hopefully."

"I'll make sure that happens."

"You don't have to," she said, laying a hand on his thigh. "Helping my parents out has been more than enough."

"I know," he said. "But I want to."

She took another sip as they sat there, quietly looking out over the water.

"What will you do when I go home?" she asked.

"Probably work more," he said.

She looked up to see a small, sad smile on his face.

"Have I been that much of a distraction?"

He looked down at her and his smile grew. "A very welcome one."

"Thank you," she said, resting her head against him.

"For everything. I can't tell you how much that means to me."

"*Amorecito, mi cielo.*"

"That sounded sexy," she said, lifting her head to look at him. "What does it mean?"

There was that devilish smirk of his. "Perhaps one day I'll tell you," he said before trying to kiss her.

She laughed, pulling away from him. "It probably means I smell like a goat or something."

"Trust me," he said, laughing with her. "You don't smell like a goat."

"And what do I smell like then?"

He set his glass down before leaning in close, pushing her hair back behind her shoulder, and this time she let him.

"You smell like citrus. And sunshine." He brushed his lips against her neck. "You smell like home," he whispered.

"Oh god," she moaned, setting her own glass down behind them. "You know just the right things to say."

"It's the truth," he said before pressing his lips to hers.

"I think it might be time to take this inside," she mumbled.

"I think you're right."

An hour later, Karina collapsed on the bed next to Damien.

"God, you're amazing," he said as he gently bit her shoulder.

"Oh no you don't," she panted.

"Don't what?" he said, propping himself up on his elbow.

"Don't you get me started already. I don't think my body could handle it yet."

"Are you saying," he kissed the top of her breast, "it

wouldn't take much?"

"Stop," she giggled.

"Only because you asked me to."

She rolled over to face him, tucking her hands under her head.

"What made you go into the coffee shop that day?" she asked. "It seems like something you'd have Tom do for you."

"Are you trying to distract me?" he asked.

"Maybe," she said with a grin, and he kissed her shoulder before answering.

"Sometimes I like to do the mundane things myself," he said. "To be around simpler people that have no idea who I am and want nothing from me. Except four dollars and eighty-five cents," he said, touching her nose.

"And next thing you know, you're bringing home one of those simpletons."

He arched an eyebrow. "I would hardly call you a simpleton. You have a bachelor's degree in public health for crying out loud," he said. "Which begs the question, what were *you* doing in that coffee shop? I would've thought there would be more prosperous options available to you."

"The plan was to keep going to school full-time," she sighed. "Get it all out of the way. I took the job because the hours were flexible and it was close to the campus. Then my mom was diagnosed with leukemia and I postponed school. I stayed at the shop because again, the hours were flexible, and I could help my dad take care of her. I'd had a scholarship—a big one. But it expired, and so now I'm starting from scratch again."

He brushed her hair back.

"Thank you," she whispered.

"For what?"

"For coming into the shop that day."

"Thank you for being there that day."

And then he kissed her with such gentleness that she could feel her heart breaking into a million pieces. Pieces she knew she was going to have to put back together someday.

"I should go," she said, pulling away from him.

"Go where?" he asked, frowning.

"To my room. It's getting late."

"Why?"

"Isn't that part of the deal? Isn't that why I have my own room?"

"Is that what you think?" he asked.

"I don't have any delusions about what this is, Damien. You don't have to worry about that."

She stood and pulled her underwear and shirt back on, picking up the rest of her clothes. It bothered her that he wasn't saying anything, just watching as she dressed, not saying the words she realized she wanted him to say. *Stay here with me.* But he didn't, and she gave him one last kiss on the cheek before heading back to her room.

Karina crawled into bed and the tears came before she could even attempt to stop them. How could she have let this happen? There were exactly thirteen days left until she went home, and Karina knew she'd better get her feelings in check if she was going to survive them.

There was a click, and she realized that the bedroom door was opening. It could only be Damien. She wiped her wet cheeks with her hands, keeping her back to the door. He crawled into the bed and pressed his naked body against her, wrapping his arm around her waist.

"I don't care if we have sex," he whispered into her ear. "Or even whose bed we're in. I just want to be close to you."

She turned in his arms to face him.

"I want to wake up next to you," he said.

"You can't say things like that," she told him.

"Why not?"

"You—you just can't."

He kissed her. Slowly and deeply, and it cut into her just as much as his words. She was standing on an edge she could never come back from, and he didn't even know he was pushing her over. But she kissed him back, knowing she didn't have the power to push him away. Didn't want to. And as he climbed on top of her, she wrapped her arms around him, her hunger for Damien growing insatiable.

As her body slowly moved with his, their lips locked together, she knew was different than all the other sex they had. It was strangely more intimate despite everything else they had already done together. Karina wanted it to end and never end at the same time. Because she was falling off the cliff. Falling quickly, and she feared there would be no one at the bottom to catch her.

Reality

SOMEONE WAS POUNDING on a door, and as Karina and Damien shot up at the sound of it, she realized it wasn't *her* door.

"Damien!" shouted Tom's voice from down the hall.

"What time is it?" Damien asked in a panic as he twisted to look at the clock. "Shit!"

"Damien, are you in there?" Tom called out.

Karina knew it wouldn't take him long to realize that Damien was *not,* in fact, in there. Because he was in here.

Damien jumped out of bed and looked around her room, completely buck-ass naked. "Shit!"

"So you slept in," she said, falling back onto the bed. "Big deal. We all do it at some point."

"*I* don't. And all my clothes are in *my* room," he pointed in the direction of it, "which Tom is standing outside of right now."

The pounding moved to her door.

"Not anymore," she said with a smile.

"Karina? Are you in there?"

"Are you going to answer it?" Damien answered.

"You're the one he's looking for."

"I'm *naked*."

"I don't see the problem here," she said with a wicked grin.

"Dammit, Karina," he seethed. "That is my employee out there. This is completely unprofessional!"

"Sorry, Mr. Bishop," she said, climbing out of bed and grabbing the robe at the end of it. "I guess I completely forgot my place."

Damien said nothing, just continued to fume.

"Karina?" Tom shouted one more time.

She simply leaned against the door, glaring at Damien. "Hey Tom, could you do me a favor and go wait downstairs?"

"I'm looking for Damien," he said. "Do you know where he is?"

"Just trust me, Tom. Go wait downstairs and I promise he will be right down."

"Oh, thank you, Karina."

"No problem."

She and Damien listened to his footsteps disappear.

"Problem solved," she said, opening the door for him and handing him the robe.

"Thank you," he muttered without much gratitude as he hastily wrapped it around himself.

She slammed the door behind him before flopping onto the bed, everything he'd said to her last night feeling like a dream.

Even though Karina had spent less than twenty-four hours in New York City, it reminded her how cold it was back home compared to sunny Miami, so she decided to take advantage of it, not having anything else to do. She spent a lot of time swimming laps in the pool, trying to burn off the frustrated energy. It sapped her energy for sure but did little for her frustration. Despite all that had happened in the past few weeks, Damien had never snapped at her.

Deciding it didn't matter—she was going home soon anyway—she laid back in a lounge chair and popped her earbuds in, letting the music soothe her wounded soul. She hadn't even realized she had dozed off until she felt something touch her leg, and she opened her eyes to see Damien sitting on the chair next to her, still dressed in a suit.

She pulled the earbuds out. "Did you need something?" she asked in an icy tone.

"I want to apologize," he said.

"Whatever for?" she said sarcastically, closing her eyes again.

"For the way I acted this morning."

"Oh, you mean when you were a complete asshole?"

"I'm sorry, Karina."

"Doesn't make it right," she said, opening her eyes.

"I know." He sighed. "It's just that—you have to understand I wasn't lying when I said I've never slept in. I've never been so caught off guard before."

She looked at him and saw the same quizzical expression she'd seen on his face that first day at the coffee shop, when he turned to look at her before walking out the door.

"You've done something to me," he said in an uncertain voice.

"Are you saying this is *my* fault?"

"No," he said quickly. "I'm just trying to explain myself. But you're right, it doesn't excuse the way I treated you." He stood up. "Come with me. I want to show you something. Please."

She climbed out of the chair and stepped into the strapless dress she had chosen as a swimsuit cover-up, curious what he had in store for her. Without a word, he led her into the house and to the front sitting room, where a beautiful cello was waiting for her next to the piano.

"What is this?" she asked.

"It's a cello," he said. "I thought that was obvious."

"I know what it is. Why is there a cello here?"

"You sounded so wistful that night, talking about playing it."

That night felt so long ago to Karina. It was hard to believe how much had happened since then.

"It's just on loan again, right?" she asked, touching the necklace still around her throat.

"You're the only person I know who plays the cello," he said. "Well, the only person I'd want to give a cello to, at least."

As Karina stood there, staring at it, her fingers started to itch, dying to touch the strings.

"Do you want to play it?" he asked.

"I don't even know if I remember any songs," she said as she sat down on the piano bench next to it.

"I think you'd be surprised," he said with a smile.

She pulled the instrument closer to her and grabbed the bow with her right hand. It felt good in her palm. Slowly she pulled it across the strings and the sound of it sent a chill down her spine. It reminded her of Damien's voice. She tried a couple chords, testing it out, and made a couple slight adjustments.

There was a song she thought she remembered. Being one of her favorites, she had played it so many times. Her fingers fell into place on the fingerboard and she bowed the strings, closing her eyes as she felt the vibrations of it. She hadn't even realized how much she missed this until now.

When the last note ended, she opened her eyes to see Damien sitting on the couch, looking awestruck.

"Vivaldi," he said and she nodded.

"From The Four Seasons."

"That was incredible."

"Thank you," she said, blushing. "It was the only song I could remember."

"It was perfect. And perhaps the next time I owe you an apology, I'll just bring home some sheet music. Any requests?"

"That you don't have to apologize to me," she said hesitantly.

"I promise to try," he said.

"That's all I ask." She stood and put the cello back on its stand. "Where are you going to keep this?" she asked.

"I think it looks nice right there next to the piano," he said, standing. "Don't you?"

"It does. And it might have to stay there, because I don't have room for this in my apartment."

He tucked her hair behind her ear. "Then I guess you'll just have to come down and play it for me from time to time," he said quietly.

Karina didn't know what to say to that. Part of her wanted to clap her hands and say yes, absolutely, but deep down she knew she could never bear it. This was going to hurt enough when she had to leave.

"What do you say we give Romi the night off and go out for dinner?" he asked.

"I'd like that," she said, forcing a smile.

They enjoyed a casual dinner (by Damien's standards) at a popular restaurant in downtown Miami. They were seated at a small table for two, and even though the place was packed, Karina felt like it was only he two of them. She barely even remembered what they ate, except for the dessert—a chocolate torte that they shared.

"Will there be anything else?" the waiter asked when he stopped by to collect the empty plate.

Damien looked at her. "Do you want anything else?" he asked.

"Nothing that's on the menu," she said with a playful smile.

"That will be all," Damien told the waiter, not taking his eyes off of her.

The waiter walked away and she excused herself to use the restroom, leaving a restless Damien at the table.

Karina was still grinning as she walked out of the bathroom—until she saw Tabitha sitting in her seat across from Damien. As she neared the table, Tabitha caught sight of her and gave Karina a nasty little smile before turning her attention back to Damien. It was all she could do not to slap the woman as Karina calmly walked over to them.

"Oh hello," Tabitha said in a sugary voice when Karina stepped up to the table to stand next to Damien. "Kari, right?"

"It's Karina, actually," Damien corrected her.

"Oops," she said with a giggle. "My mistake."

"So what brings you to our table?" Karina asked, attempting her best smile.

"Well, I was attending a private function in the back room. Gregson's birthday in fact," said Tabitha, shooting a glance at Damien. "And I happened to catch a glimpse of Damien out here. I thought what kind of friend would I be if I didn't stop by and say hi?"

"What kind of friend indeed," said Karina.

Damien covered his mouth as he gave a little cough, and though he was suppressing a smile behind that hand, Karina could see it in his eyes.

"By the way," Karina said, shifting closer to Damien. "I wanted to tell you that you were wrong about the museum gala last weekend."

"Is that so?" Tabitha asked with a frown.

"Yes, I didn't find it boring at all." Karina rested her hand on Damien's shoulder, and she felt his hand on her lower back. "In fact, I think it was the most fun I've ever had at an event." She looked down at Damien who was holding his chin, focusing on the table. "Wouldn't you agree?"

He raised his eyes to her, trying not to laugh. "I'd have to agree one hundred percent."

The waiter came back with Damien's credit card and the slip for him to sign.

"I'm glad to hear that," Tabitha said, though she clearly wasn't.

"It's been a pleasure as always, Tabitha," Damien sighed, sliding the card back into his wallet. "But Karina and I are going to head home now."

"It's so early, though," she pouted. "You really should come join the party in the back. And Karina, obviously."

"Obviously," Damien muttered. "I appreciate the invite," he said, "However—"

"Damien Bishop!" someone shouted, and Karina and Damien both turned around so see a man coming their way. "I thought that was you," he said, shaking Damien's hand. "What are you doing here?"

"Gregson," said Damien. "We were just having dinner."

"And who might you be?" Gregson asked, flashing Karina a toothy smile as he extended his hand.

"Karina," she said, accepting it before shifting closer to Damien as she noticed Tabitha rolling her eyes.

"Pleasure to meet you." Gregson turned back to Damien. "How are you, man?"

"I'm good," said Damien. "And yourself?"

"Couldn't be better. It's my birthday party going on

back there."

"So I heard. Happy birthday," said Damien.

"You should come have a drink with me. We haven't talked in forever."

"Thank you, but Karina and I were about to head home."

"Oh, come on," said Gregson. "One drink. You aren't going to say no to the birthday boy, are you?"

Damien sighed but smiled.

"No," he said. "Of course not."

"Excellent."

Damien took Karina's hand, and the four of them walked into the private room in the back.

"There's a good reason why he and I haven't talked in a while," Damien whispered to her. "We won't be staying long."

The private room was packed with people. In the center was a table laid out with food, and a small bar lined the back wall.

Tabitha mingled back into the crowd while Karina and Damien followed Gregson to the bar.

"Can I get three shots of Patron?" Gregson asked the bartender.

"None for me, please," Karina said. Straight tequila was the last thing she needed.

"Come on," said Gregson. "It's just one shot."

"She said no," Damien told him firmly.

Gregson frowned but turned to the bartender and told him only two.

"Is there something else you would like?" Damien asked.

"Water would be nice," she said, and Damien requested it.

Damien lifted his glass to Gregson. "Happy birthday."

"To old times," said Gregson, and Karina caught the

look in Damien's face. He didn't care for this man any more than she did.

Word got around that Damien was in the room, and everyone wanted to say hi. He introduced her to most people, but it was obvious they were more interested in him, so she wandered off, content to just people-watch. As she stood in the corner, sipping her water, Tabitha sidled up next to her.

"So who are you, exactly?" she asked.

"Um, Karina Watson."

Tabitha rolled her eyes. "How do you know Damien?" she asked. "What's your angle?"

"I don't have an angle," Karina told her. "And how I know Damien is none of your business."

Tabitha moved so that she was now standing face to face with Karina.

"Everyone knows that Damien is the most eligible bachelor around. You can't honestly think some nobody like you is going to land him."

"First of all, I'm not trying to *land* him. But if I was," Karina gave her a patronizing smile, "I'm pretty sure my odds are way better than yours."

Tabitha narrowed her eyes. "You little—"

"Ahem."

Tabitha turned around to find Damien right behind her.

"Do you mind if I borrow Karina for a moment?"

"Oh, of course," Tabitha said in the fake sweet voice of hers. "We were just having a friendly little chat."

"I'm sure you were," he said as he reached for Karina's hand, pulled her into him, and led her out of the room. "What was she saying to you?" he asked.

"Apparently you're the most eligible bachelor around," she told him.

He chuckled, shaking his head. "Let's get out of here."

Damien handed his ticket to the valet and then turned to

Karina while they waited.

"Is there anything else you want to do before we head home?" he asked.

"I don't know. Any suggestions?"

He stepped closer and wrapped a tendril of her hair around his finger.

"I suggest," he said, "that we head back to the house and spend the rest of the evening tangled up in each other."

The door behind him opened, and out of the corner of her eye, Karina recognized Tabitha walking out of it.

"I think," Karina said, pressing her chest against Damien's, "that's a splendid idea."

A smile spread across his face as he lowered his lips to Karina's mouth.

The valet attendant returned with Damien's car and he released her. Karina caught the look on Tabitha's face just before the vile woman walked back into the restaurant.

She knew it was petty, but Karina couldn't help the feeling of satisfaction as she slid into the Mercedes.

"Why do you even bother with her?" Karina asked as Damien drove.

"Excuse me?"

"Tabitha. Why do you allow her to think you two are friends? Why not tell her to, well, to fuck off?"

He laughed. "Trust me, I've been tempted to. Especially tonight," he said, taking Karina's hand and kissing it.

"Then why don't you? Why the charade?"

"That's just the way it is with these people," he sighed. "We all pretend to get along to get what we want. Take Gregson for example. Two years ago, he poached one of my best VPs. Then three months later, he let the guy go."

"Did you hire him back?"

"I couldn't trust him after that. Meanwhile, Gregson acts like it's water under the bridge. Unfortunately, his security systems run off our software, so I have to act like it as well."

"But what about Tabitha? What does she offer you?"

"Tabitha is a gossip who runs in a lot of the same circles. I stay on her good side to keep the rumors to a minimum."

"It seemed like you were doing more than staying on her good side at the engagement party."

Damien looked at her with a sheepish smile.

"I have a confession to make," he said. "I was trying to make you jealous."

Karina's hand flew out at his chest before she even realized what she was doing.

"Ouch," he groaned, rubbing his chest. "You know, it's not smart to attack the driver while he's driving."

"I can't believe you," she said, massaging her hand. She'd forgotten how solid his chest was.

"I'm sorry," he said, reaching for the hand that had just assaulted him. "It was childish. I didn't know how else to get your attention."

"That's the second time you've apologized to me today."

"Does is still count if I'm apologizing for something that happened over a week ago?"

"I think that makes it worse."

"I'm really sorry, Karina. Can you forgive me?"

She thought about that night and how jealous she had in fact been, even if she hadn't been willing to admit it. And it was that jealousy that had sent her into Damien's bedroom after the party. He'd manipulated her, and Karina wanted to be mad at him. But as she looked at him glancing her way, waiting for her forgiveness, she knew she wouldn't have been jealous if she hadn't felt something for him. And wasn't she just as guilty of trying to manipulate him once she knew what he was trying to do?

"No more tricks," she said. "No more games."

"Agreed," he said, giving her hand a squeeze.

The next several days flew by, no matter how much Karina wanted time to slow down. Damien worked as little as possible, retreating only to his home office when necessary. And there were no more business trips, despite what the itinerary said.

Tom still stopped by most days to check in with Damien, and Karina could sense his irritation at the whole situation, even though he said nothing to her.

As the last day drew closer, Karina wondered how she was supposed to say goodbye. She wondered if Damien even wanted to.

Her room was rarely used anymore—it was mostly just a place to keep her clothes. Even some of those had migrated into Damien's closet out of convenience.

And before she knew it, her last weekend in Miami had arrived.

Damien had to go into work for a few hours that Saturday but was back before noon.

"What do you say we go grab lunch somewhere near the beach?"

"I like that idea," she said, and the two of them headed out in Damien's Porsche. They enjoyed a leisurely lunch at a bistro on the water, and when he finally paid the bill, Damien invited her to walk with him along the boardwalk.

"I have something I want to talk to you about," he said.

"Okay," she replied, worried what it could be.

He took her hand and led her out to the crowded pavement. Of course everyone was spending Saturday afternoon at the beach. They walked for several minutes and he still had not said anything.

"What is it you wanted to talk to me about?" she asked, hoping she didn't regret pushing him.

"I wanted to ask you about the graduate program you're applying for."

"Oh. Okay, what about it?"

"I'm curious why you chose—"

Just then, someone in a jacket and ball cap rushed past them, bumping his shoulder into Damien.

"Excuse me," Damien said, even though it wasn't his fault. The guy seemed not to have noticed, and they continued walking.

"I wanted to ask—"

"Damien Bishop!"

Damien and Karina both turned around to see the same guy facing them, holding a gun, and while Karina would later remember it as having happened so fast, everything slowed down as she registered the gun and Damien's men rushing toward the attacker. And then all at once Damien was stepping in front of her at the same moment the bodyguards reached the man—just as shot went off and Karina was knocked off her feet by Damien falling against her. She managed to land on her ass, but Damien was on his back next to her, blood soaking the left corner of his shirt.

"Oh my god, Damien!" she said, leaning over him. "Damien!" She looked around to see that most people had hit the ground at the sound of the gunshot, but some people were still standing, coming closer now that Damien's men were on the attacker, securing his hands.

"Someone call 911!" she screamed but quickly realized that one of Damien's bodyguards was already on the phone.

"Damien," she said, looking down at him with tears in her eyes.

"It's okay," he said through gritted teeth.

"Okay? Damien, you've been shot!"

He lifted his head enough to look down and see the red

staining his clothes. "So I have," he said. "That's annoying."

She laughed, which only made her cry more. "Stop being such an ass," she said. "This is serious. Don't you die on me."

"At least your beautiful face would be the last thing I see."

"Shut up," she scolded. "I would punch you if you weren't shot."

"I appreciate the restraint," he said. "Honestly, I don't think it's that bad."

He tried to sit up, but Karina stopped him.

"You are not moving until help gets here," she told him, taking his hand.

"How long is that going to take?" he asked just as one of Damien's men came over, still on the phone.

"EMTs are on their way, sir," he said. "We aren't far from the nearest hospital, so it shouldn't be too long."

"Good," said Damien with a nod as he squeezed Karina's hand.

He seemed fine, but all the blood terrified Karina, and she worried that he was in shock.

Damien's bodyguard was right, and sirens could soon be heard. It wasn't long before paramedics and police officers were pushing through the crowd. One officer pulled Karina to the side while the medics attended to Damien. She answered their questions as best she could—there wasn't much to say—and watched as Damien was put on a stretcher and wheeled to the ambulance.

"Where are they taking him?" she asked the officer. "Can I go with him?"

The officer nodded, and Karina rushed to the ambulance.

"Can I go with him?" she repeated to the medic as he was about to step into the vehicle.

"Are you his wife?" he asked.

"No, but I'm—" She didn't have an answer for him. Girlfriend didn't sound like the right word either.

"She's with me," Damien said from inside, and the medic helped her in.

"Is he going to be okay?" she asked, taking Damien's hand again.

"We'll know more when we get to the hospital," said the EMT, keeping pressure on the upper left side of his chest.

Karina frowned.

"It's fine," Damien said.

The sirens came on again as the ambulance started moving, and Karina gave a little prayer, hoping that he really was fine.

Final Days

IT DIDN'T TAKE long for them to get to the hospital, and Karina was left at the front desk while they wheeled Damien into a room.

"Karina!"

She spun around to see Tom walking through the doors.

"Is he okay?" he asked.

"I don't know," she said. "They aren't telling me much. Damien insists he's fine."

"Of course he does."

A nurse walked up to them carrying a clipboard.

"Is one of you able to fill out paperwork for Mr. Bishop?" she asked.

"I've got it," Tom said, taking the board and pen.

He and Karina moved over to some nearby chairs.

"What happened?" Tom asked.

"I don't know," she said. "We were just walking when some random guy pulled a gun on us. He shouted Damien's name, though, so he obviously knew him."

The police officers from the scene walked in, accompanied by Damien's security, and one of them pointed in their direction.

"Will you hold this for a second?" Tom asked, handing her the clipboard.

Karina took the paperwork and watched with curiosity as Tom walked up to them and they all moved into a corner to talk. After what felt like forever, Tom returned and the cops headed down the same direction Damien had been taken.

"Is everything okay?" she asked Tom.

"Yeah, it's fine. That was a close call," he said. "How are you doing?"

"I'm terrified," she replied, staring at nothing. "I'm in shock. Mostly I'm just worried about Damien."

"You and me both," Tom said as he continued filling out the forms.

"I think I'm falling for him, Tom," she sighed, and he sucked in a breath.

"You can't say anything," he said. "I like you Karina, I really do. And that's why I'm warning you that this can't end well."

"I know," she muttered.

"I'm the closest thing he has to a friend, and I can tell you that Damien Bishop doesn't do…*that*. I'm not even sure if he's capable of it."

"You can't mean that."

"He's too jaded. He's spent his life surrounded by fake, superficial people. People who only want to be around you if you have something to benefit them."

"Sounds like he's not the only one who's jaded."

"It's our world," Tom said with a shrug. "Even if I don't have Damien's money, I see what it does to people. How it shows their true colors."

Karina leaned her head on Tom's shoulder. "I don't care about his money. I just want him to be okay."

"I know," he said. "Me too."

Tom let her sit like that for a while until a doctor came out.

"You can see him now," she said and led them to one of the rooms.

Damien was sitting shirtless on a table with bandaging around his left arm.

"He's free to go home," the doctor said before walking out.

"Wait," Karina called after her. "That's it? He's been shot and you're sending him home already?"

"It was just a graze," Damien said, starting to put the bloody shirt back on, then thinking twice about it. "Tom, will you find a shop or something nearby and get me a clean shirt?"

"On it," Tom said and walked out of the room.

Damien jumped off the table and threw the shirt in the bin marked "biological hazards."

"Just a graze?" Karina asked. "But there was so much blood. And why were you in here for so long?"

"The bullet managed to nick a vein. They stopped the bleeding quickly enough, but they wanted to make sure I wasn't light-headed before they let me go."

"And here I was sick with worry out there."

He touched her cheek. "You weren't really that worried about me, were you?"

"Of course I was! Damien, I watched a man shoot you."

His face went dark. "I'm just glad he didn't hit anyone else. Especially you."

"Who is he? The police asked me a couple questions, but they seemed to get everything they needed from your security team. I noticed they even spoke with Tom."

"He was a stalker."

"You have a stalker?" she asked.

"Yes and no. He's been stalking this model who I happened to accompany to an event once. Our picture was in some tabloid and he started sending me threatening letters, accusing me of stealing his girlfriend. My men looked into it and he didn't seem like a real threat. But I guess he had a psychotic break recently and for some reason blamed me."

"Oh my god, Damien, that's messed up."

"And that's why I have security."

"But this man still shot you."

"And he probably would have succeeded in killing me if it hadn't been for them." He frowned. "Or you. I'm just sorry that you were in harm's way."

"What happened last time?" she asked. "You said something had happened once before. Was that a stalker as well?"

He shook his head. "It was a cousin."

"A cousin," she repeated, wide-eyed.

"After my parents died, she apparently felt slighted for being left out of the will, even though we'd never had much contact with her. She tried to sabotage my car, thinking that if I died, she would inherit everything. Fortunately, she not only did a horrible job of executing the plan, but she left so much evidence that there was no doubt who it was. And the irony of it was that if anything had happened to me, a little would have gone to staff, but the bulk of it is set up to go to various charities."

"I'm so sorry," Karina said.

"Don't worry about it," he said, shrugging. "Like I said, I never really knew her. Now she's just my crazy cousin."

"Where is she now?"

"Serving a life sentence in prison."

"That's awful," she said, crossing her arms.

Tom walked in carrying a plastic bag. "I managed to

find a t-shirt in the gift shop," he said.

Damien pulled out the navy blue t-shirt that said Miami, FL across the chest.

"It was the plainest thing they had," Tom explained.

"I just need it to get me home."

Apparently word had gotten out that an attempt had been made on Damien Bishop's life, because as they neared the glass entrance doors of the hospital, news teams could be seen waiting outside.

"I've got this," Tom said. "You go out a side entrance and have security pick you up. I'll meet you back at the house."

"What's he doing?" Karina asked as Damien led her through the hospital, looking for a door that wasn't being watched.

"He's giving a statement on my behalf," he said. "I'm not a fan of talking to the press in the first place, and the last thing I need is footage of me in this awful t-shirt on the nightly news."

"I kinda like the t-shirt," she said with a smirk.

"It's a little tight," he grumbled.

"Exactly."

He looked at her and smiled just as they found an exit. His bodyguards found them quickly and dropped them off at the restaurant where Damien's car was still waiting.

Karina couldn't believe how late it was by the time they got back to the house. Now that Damien was safe and well, she felt cheated. In less than forty-eight hours, she was heading home.

"How exactly am I getting home on Monday?" she asked hesitantly when they sat down to dinner.

"The same way you arrived here," he said.

"Your plane?"

He nodded. "Is that all right?"

"Of course."

"Um, what time?"

"I told Jim he should plan take-off for eleven," he told her. "That way he can get back at a decent hour."

"That sounds fair," she said, pushing the food on her plate around.

"Are you that eager to leave now that I've put you in danger?" he said in jest, but she could see the uncertainty in his eyes.

"What? You didn't put me in danger."

"A man fired a gun at us today, Karina. It could have just as easily hit you instead of me."

"That's not your fault," she said. While it wasn't a pleasant topic, at least they weren't discussing her homecoming any longer.

He grabbed her hand resting on the table.

"I don't know what I would have done if something had happened to you," he said.

"Well, I was a mess earlier because something *did* happen to you," she said, squeezing his hand. "I'm glad you're okay though."

"I'm beginning to feel invincible," he said with a smile.

"It's thoughts like those that will get you killed," she said, not returning his smile.

"Good advice. Now why don't we talk about something else. Like why you aren't touching your food."

Karina looked down at her plate. "I'm not hungry, I guess."

Once Romi cleared the plates, Karina tried to talk Damien into a night-time swim, but he wouldn't hear it for fear of what his men might witness. She let him convince her to watch a movie in the entertainment room. It was the most normal—mundane, as Damien might say—activity, but Karina cherished being curled up in his lap, the two of them just being together. It only lasted halfway through the movie, though, since it turned out they couldn't keep their hands off of each other for that long, and they eventually moved up into the bedroom.

Karina fell asleep that night with Damien at her back, his arms wrapped tightly around her, and she wished he never had to let go.

Karina woke the next morning, aware that it was her last full day here. Damien was still asleep, his back to her, and she faced it, pressing her lips to his warm skin. He stirred and she ran a hand down his back and around to the front of him.

"Are you trying to start something?" he murmured, rolling onto his back.

"Only if you want me to," she said, climbing on top of him.

He smiled as he ran a hand up her arm to the base of her neck.

"I always want you to," he said, sitting up so that she was now in his lap.

Karina stared into his honey-colored eyes, so many things she wanted to say on the tip of her tongue, yet she was unable to say them. She settled on kissing him, pressing her chest against his as though her heart could speak to his. He responded by wrapping his arms around her, pulling her into him so tight it was difficult to breathe. And still it wasn't enough.

They finally dressed and headed downstairs for breakfast, but he pulled her in the opposite direction of the dining room.

"There's something I want to show you," he said, leading her into his office, where he sat in the chair at his desk.

He pulled her into his lap and tapped the touch pad, bringing the screen to life and revealing a web page.

"What's this?" she asked, scanning the page.

"Read it," he said. "This is what I was going to talk to you about yesterday on the boardwalk."

"Miller School of Medicine? Where's that?"

"It's here," he said. "At the University of Miami."

"Why are you showing me this?"

"I thought you might be interested in going to school down here. It's a great program. It ranks—"

"Why do you think I should go to school here instead?" she asked, looking him in the face.

Say it, Damien. Just say it.

"I just thought you might not be ready to go home yet," he said quietly.

"There's a huge difference between not being ready to go home and committing to two years of school down here."

"You're saying you don't want to stay?"

"I'm saying that my family is up north. I'd need a reason to stay."

His eyes searched her face.

Dammit, Damien, just say it, she screamed in her head.

His lips parted, about to say something, and her heart raced.

"I understand," he said, and her face fell. "That makes sense."

"Does it?" she asked, frowning at him.

He nodded. "What shall we do for your last day, then?"

And there went the last little thread holding her heart together. It was all she could do not to run off to the bedroom and cry. But she wasn't about to waste her last few moments with Damien. Even if he was willing to let her go.

"Will you take me out on the boat? One last time," she said, almost choking on the words.

He grazed her cheek. "Of course."

They boarded the boat with a full basket of wine and food, compliments of Romi. Damien let her take the helm again, and again they ended up down below, all the while those depressing words hovering in the back of Karina's mind. *One last time*.

When they both became too restless to lie in bed any more, Damien led her back up top, where they set out a blanket and watched the sun set over the city of Miami.

"Have you ever watched a sunset on the west coast?" he asked as she leaned back into him.

"I've never even left *this* coast," she said.

"It sets on the ocean over there. It's beautiful."

"Maybe someday I'll get the chance."

He kissed the top of her head while grazing the fingers of his right hand along her left arm. Neither said anything more until the sun slipped down below the buildings and only the orange glow was left.

"We should probably head back in," he finally said. "I'm not too keen on docking in the darkness."

She turned around to face him.

"What if we just sailed away forever?" she asked. "We could be nomads, going wherever the wind takes us."

He smiled at her.

"Then you'd really never finish school," he said.

"It was a thought."

"A very nice one." He brushed a stay hair from her face. "Stand up, I need your help."

Together they sailed the boat the short distance back home, where someone was waiting to assist Damien in tying it off.

When that was done, she and Damien walked up to the house, where a candlelit dinner was set up on the patio.

"Oh, Damien," Karina breathed.

"I wanted to make sure your last night was

memorable," he said.

She turned to face him.

"This whole month has been memorable."

"I'm glad you came down," he whispered as he touched his forehead to hers.

"Me too."

That night, Karina found Damien to be just as reluctant to fall asleep as she was. Even after they were too exhausted for sex, they continued to lie there, talking about everything except what tomorrow would bring.

When the alarm went off the next morning, Karina was sure she had just closed her eyes and wanted nothing more than to spend every last second in bed with Damien. He must have been thinking the same thing, because he climbed out of bed and opened the door, where a breakfast tray was waiting.

"I thought this would save time," he said, setting it on the bed between him and her where they ate breakfast, completely naked.

"What time does the car arrive?" she asked, glancing at the clock.

"A little less than an hour," he said sadly.

"I should probably get in the shower, then."

He nodded.

"Care to join me?" she asked.

"Wouldn't miss it for the world," he said with a smirk.

Eventually she was dressed and stuffing the last few items into her toiletry bag.

"Car's here," Damien said. "I'll take your suitcases downstairs."

"Okay, I'll be right down."

Damien walked up to her and held her face in his hands before kissing her. It was beautiful, and she felt a tear slide down her cheek knowing this kiss was among the last.

When he pulled away, he looked into her eyes as he wiped the tear with his thumb. And then he turned around to walk out.

Karina gripped the counter, needing a second to collect herself. Taking a deep, calming breath, she grabbed her toiletry bag and shoved it into the duffle still on the bed. She made her way down the stairs to find only Tom in the foyer with her bags, typing away on his phone.

"Ready to go?" he asked, looking up.

"I think so. Where's Damien?"

"He, uh, he's in his office. Should we get going?"

"What about Damien?"

Tom's face fell. "I'm sorry Karina. I tried to warn you."

"You mean he's not coming with? He's not even going to say goodbye?"

Tom shook his head, looking at her with pity.

Karina dropped her bag and stormed off.

"Karina! I don't think—"

"Shut up, Tom!"

She didn't even bother knocking on the door, just barged in.

"You can't even fucking say goodbye?"

Damien was sitting in the small sofa against a wall, his head in his hands, but he looked up at her, his eyes red.

She rushed over and knelt before him, placing her hands on his knees.

"I want to stay, Damien. I really do. But I need to know I'm doing it for a damn good reason."

"What do you want me to say?" he asked, his voice cracking.

"Tell me why you want me to stay. Why were you asking me to go to school in Miami?"

"I want you here. Isn't that enough?"

"But *why* do you want me here? Why did you come to my apartment that morning? Why did you pull so many strings just to bring me down here?"

"I can't tell you what you want to hear," he said, slowly shaking his head. "I don't know if I ever will."

She stood up. "Then I can't stay here." Tears trickled down her cheeks as she reached up to unclasp the necklace.

"Don't," he said. "I want you to keep it."

"I don't want the trinket of a man too damn chicken to speak his heart."

Her hand trembled as she held it out to him, but he refused to accept it.

"Take it, Damien."

"No," he whispered.

She slammed it on the side table and made her way to the door.

"It's not like you've said it!" he called out, and she turned around. "We both know you're just as stubborn as I am. You can't say it either."

"I love you, Damien. Is that what you've been waiting for? I. Love. You."

He looked at her, anguish in his eyes, but still he said nothing.

"Goodbye, Damien."

She slammed the door behind her and marched into the foyer, where Tom was still waiting with her bags.

"Let's go," she snapped, walking right past him and out the front door.

Home

KARINA BOARDED THE plane and threw her purse on a seat before dropping into the one across from it. Then she realized it was the same two seats she and Damien had always sat in, so she got up and stormed to another one.

"Can I get you anything?" Tom asked hesitantly.

"A stiff drink," she said, staring out the window.

"Any preference?"

She turned to look at him.

"You know what, never mind. I don't want anything else from him. Just get me home."

"It's a three-hour flight," he said. "Sure you don't want a snack or something?"

Karina narrowed her eyes at him, and Tom finally turned without saying anything to take a seat on the opposite side of the cabin. She looked out the window again, feeling guilty about her rudeness. He had tried to warn her, after all. What made her think that she knew

Damien better than Tom?

The plane was at cruising altitude before Karina turned around.

"I'm sorry," she said. "I didn't meant to snap at you."

"Apology accepted," he said. "Not that I really blame you."

Karina faced the seat in front of her again for a second before twisting back around.

"You probably get yelled at a lot, don't you?" she said. "By the exes, I mean."

Tom raised an eyebrow at her.

"What?" she asked.

"You're the first," he said.

Confused, she climbed out of her seat and sat across from Tom.

"People keep saying that," she said. "That I'm the first. Surely Damien's dated others."

Tom frowned, clearly uncomfortable with the topic, and she rolled her eyes.

"I'm not asking for details, or even names. But you can't honestly tell me he's never dated anyone else."

"He has," Tom said, still scowling. "Never anything serious though. Not like you."

"I suppose I was a trial run then," she said, crossing her arms.

"I told you—"

"I know," she said, uncrossing her arms and standing up. "Damien Bishop doesn't do love."

She settled back into her seat and didn't speak another word for the rest of the flight.

It was raining when the plane landed, and Karina felt like the city was crying for her, as if it felt her pain. She dug a rain jacket out of her bag as the door was opened and Tom escorted her under an umbrella out to the waiting town car.

"I can ride with you to your apartment," he said as the driver loaded her bags.

"It's okay," she told him. "You might as well head home."

"I'm sor—"

"Don't," she snapped, and Tom shut his mouth. "Don't you dare apologize for him."

He sighed. "Goodbye, Karina."

"Bye, Tom."

"Oh, I can't believe I almost forgot!" He pulled an envelope from his inside jacket pocket and handed it to her.

"What's this?" she asked.

"It's your tuition. As per the agreement, I believe."

"I don't think I want this anymore," she said with a frown.

"Just take it," said Tom. "Think of what this can do for your future."

Her future without Damien.

And then, to her surprise, he pulled her into a hug.

"Good luck," he whispered.

"Thank you."

She stuffed the envelope in her purse and climbed into the car while Tom watched. It wasn't until she was pulling away that he finally turned to re-board the plane.

The rain had subsided by the time the car pulled up to the building, and the driver offered to carry the bags for her, but she declined. Time to get used to doing things herself again.

As he pulled away, she stared up at the drab brick building. The whole block looked gray compared to what she had just left behind.

The apartment was empty since Ginny was still at work, and Karina dragged her bags into the bedroom that she didn't remember being so tiny. How could one month have changed her perception so drastically? She sunk onto her bed and took a deep breath before lying back onto the pillow, curling into a ball. Instinctively she reached for her neck only to be reminded that the necklace was no longer there. A sob caught in her throat, but she sat up, fighting it back. She needed to do something. She wasn't going to sit here and cry over him. Damien didn't deserve any more of her time.

The newest suitcase, a Louis Vuitton courtesy of Damien, was packed full of the clothes and shoes she had been showered with while in Miami. She shoved this suitcase in the corner of her closet without even opening it and worked at putting her real life back where it belonged. She was putting away the last of her items when she heard the key in the door and braced herself to face Ginny.

Karina walked into the living room just as Ginny closed the door.

"Karina!" she squealed, dropping her bag onto the floor and hugging Karina. "When did you get home?"

"About an hour ago," Karina muttered into her ear.

Ginny released her and pulled her over to the couch. "You have to tell me everything!" Ginny jumped up. "Wait, let me grab the wine. You wouldn't believe the day I've had at work," she said, heading into the kitchen. "This is exactly what I need to take my mind off of it."

Karina sat on the couch staring at her hands while Ginny poured two glasses and walked back in with them.

"Did you have an amazing time?" she asked, handing Karina a glass. "I bet you didn't want to come home."

Karina put a hand over her face, unable to stop the tears.

"What's wrong?" Ginny asked, taking the glass back and setting it on the coffee table. "Karina, what happened?"

"I fell in love with him," Karina managed to choke out.

"You what? I don't understand. I thought nothing was

going on between you two."

Karina shook her head, trying to wipe away some of the tears.

"Why didn't you tell me?" Ginny asked, frowning.

"Because I didn't know what to say. I wasn't sure I understood what was happening."

"You mean you did sleep with him?"

Karina nodded.

"You lied to me?"

"No!" Karina said. "Nothing happened in the beginning."

"I'm so confused," Ginny said, shaking her head.

"Join the club," Karina said, grabbing her wine from the table and taking a swig.

"So you're in love with him now, even though you didn't want to go with him in the first place." Karina nodded. "But he doesn't feel the same even though he's the one who dragged you down there?"

"I don't know," Karina mumbled.

"What do you mean?"

"I think—I think he feels the same about me. He wanted me to go to school down there."

Ginny started rubbing her temple. "I don't understand what the problem is then."

"Apparently he doesn't believe in love," Karina said bitterly. "And I won't uproot my life for a man who isn't entirely sure what he wants."

"Cheers to that," Ginny said with a sympathetic smile.

Karina tilted her glass toward Ginny before downing the last of the wine.

"I need a shower," she said, taking her glass to the kitchen sink. "And then I'm crawling into bed. I already called the shop to let them know I'm back, and they want me to open tomorrow."

"Are you sure that's a good idea?" Ginny asked.

"What am I supposed to do?"

"Maybe take a day or two. Wait until you feel better."

"He already took thirty days from me," said Karina. "I'm not giving him any more."

"Okay," Ginny said softly, nodding.

Karina took her shower and crawled into bed, where she didn't get much sleep. She never imagined how much she would miss sharing a bed with someone. With Damien.

The first day back at work went just as Karina expected—long and miserable. Everyone kept commenting on her tan, but thanks to the cloud of melancholy surrounding her, no one questioned if she had really been dealing with a family emergency.

There were only fifteen minutes left until she could head home to crawl back under her covers when her father walked in.

"Dad!" she said, walking up to him from where she had been restocking the creamers and napkins. "What are you doing here?"

"Your mother said she got a text saying you were back," he said. "Was hoping you and I could talk."

"Of course. I'm off soon, but let me see if I can clock out early."

Since it was slow and Michael believed her to still be grieving—technically she was, just not in the way everyone suspected—he gave her the okay. She grabbed her stuff and walked out with her dad.

"There's a park around the corner," he said. "Why don't we find a bench there."

"All right."

Karina followed him, nervous about what they would say to each other. Other than the text she sent her mom last night, she hadn't really spoken to her parents since New York.

"Why did you really go to Miami?" he asked once they were seated. "Was it because of Damien Bishop?"

She nodded.

"You weren't working for the coffee shop then?"

"No," she said, slumping her shoulders.

"Why did you lie to us? Why the secrecy? And why the hell did that man pay all our bills?"

Karina sighed. "I really did meet him at the coffee shop—that part was true. Up here though. He asked me out and I said no."

"So when you didn't want to," her father said, his face reddening, "he decided to bribe you?"

"I did want to, though," she told him. "I wanted to say yes. But I told him I had to say no because I had too much going on right now. Between mom and work and trying to go back to school…."

"Sweetie, have you been putting your life on hold this whole time?"

She shrugged. "I wanted to be there for you guys."

"Oh Karina, I had no idea. Your mother and I never wanted that for you."

"Damien offered to help. Except instead of dinner, he requested I stay with him for a month in exchange."

"And you didn't find that alarming?" her father asked with a frown.

"I did," she said. "But I didn't think it was something he could possibly pull off. I agreed, thinking the whole thing was a joke. The next day I realized what a fool I was and decided to contact him and say never mind." She looked down at her hands. "But before I got a chance, mom called. And she was so happy."

"She was, wasn't she," her father said, and she looked up at him. "It was like a huge burden had been lifted off her shoulders."

"I decided a month was nothing compared to what you

two had been through the past year."

"You can't really think that," he said, disgusted.

"It wasn't like that though," she said, raising her eyebrows. "Damien was a complete gentleman. I had my own room and was free to do whatever I wanted."

"Why did he take you down there then?"

"Honestly, I'm not sure. To get to know me better, I suppose." She could feel the lump forming in her throat.

"Are you going to see him again?" Ron asked.

Karina shook her head, tears threatening to spill.

"He let me go, Dad. I fell in love with him, and he let me go when the month was over."

Ron wrapped an arm around her shoulder. "That's no gentleman, Sweetie."

Neither of them said anything while she cried on her father's shoulder. Finally, Karina sat up and wiped her eyes.

"Enough of this," she said. "I'm done crying over him."

"That's my girl," said Ron, but with a frown.

Karina hugged her father.

"And I'm sorry I called you a…," he said as she pulled away. "I'm sorry for what I said in New York."

"It's okay," she told him. "I should've told you what was really going on."

They stood, and Karina walked him to his car.

"Do me a favor," Ron said as he unlocked it.

"What's that?"

"Don't forget to live your life. I know how easy it is to wait until things get better. But if you wait too long, you might miss out on some amazing stuff."

"Thanks for the advice," she said with a smile.

"Anytime," he said. "And don't be afraid to talk to us."

"I won't. Not anymore. I promise."

She hugged him one more time and watched him drive away before walking back to her apartment.

For the next two days, Karina managed not to lose it, despite the tears constantly threatening to spill. But then came her first day off since getting back, and she discovered what a distraction work had been.

It was a weekday, so even Ginny wasn't around to keep Karina's mind off Damien. She just needed time to dull the pain, and rather than sit around all day, she headed out to the library to print out the application forms now that funding her education was a sure thing.

As she waited impatiently for the printer to spit out the papers, she wondered how difficult it would be to get through school knowing that he had made it possible.

It wouldn't have to be, she realized. The cashier's check for tuition was still in her purse. She could send it back and revert to her original plan of scholarships and working it off herself. Surely the offer to move back in with her parents still stood. And then she remembered why her parents were able to make that offer.

"Dammit," she muttered, grabbing the stack of papers. Reminders of Damien were everywhere.

She took the scenic route home, and as she walked into her apartment, her phone started ringing. Karina didn't recognize the number, but she knew the area code was Miami.

"Hello?" she asked cautiously.

"Karina. It's Tom."

"Tom? Is everything okay?" Panic swept through her. "Did something happen to Damien?"

"No, no, no. Damien's fine. Well, sort of."

"What do you mean?" she asked.

"I'm sorry, Karina. I was wrong."

"What are you talking about?"

"I was wrong," he repeated. "I was wrong about how he felt. I never imagined—"

"Tom, what the hell is going on?" she asked, dropping onto the couch. "Why are you calling me?"

"Damien's been a mess ever since you left. He's completely unhinged. He's unproductive and keeps snapping at everyone to do their jobs." He paused and took a deep breath before continuing. "I don't think he's sleeping."

"What do you want me to do about it?" she asked.

"I think you should come back. Or at least call him."

"Does he know you're calling me?"

"God no. He'd probably fire me if he knew I was talking to you."

"Where is he now?"

"He's outside. Just sitting on that damn boat, doing nothing."

She massaged her forehead. "I don't know what to tell you, Tom."

"You could make this better, Karina. You can fix him."

"He knows what he needs to do if he wants me to come back," she said. "It's easy."

"Not for him."

"Tough shit. If it's important enough, if *I'm* important enough, he'll find a way to say the words."

"I don't think he knows how to."

"I can't do this, Tom."

"Karina—"

"I need you not to call me anymore." She hung up the phone and broke down all over again.

"Have you decided what you're going to wear?" Ginny asked, peeking her head in Karina's room.

"No," Karina groaned from where she was lying lengthwise across her bed. "I changed my mind, I'm not going out."

"Yes you are," Ginny said as she walked in and started

rifling through Karina's closet. "It's Saturday night and you can't just hang out here by yourself."

"I do it all the time."

Ginny sighed as she stopped what she was doing and came to sit on the bed.

"I think it will be good for you to get out," she said in a soothing voice. "You're just going to make yourself more miserable by sitting here wallowing in it."

Karina forced herself to sit up. "You're right."

"Yay!" Ginny cheered, giving her a hug.

The idea of socializing did not appeal to Karina at all, but Ginny did her best to keep the mood upbeat as they got ready, and by the time they walked out the door an hour later, Karina felt her spirits improving.

The two of them were halfway down the stairs, laughing at something Ginny had said, when someone walked in the building entrance, causing Karina to stop short.

"What's the—" but Ginny didn't have to finish when she saw who had come in.

"What are you doing here?" Karina asked Damien, who was standing at the door, looking up at her.

"I need to talk to you," he said.

Karina's heart raced. There was only one reason he would come all this way to talk to her.

"I was just headed out," she said, not willing to make it easy for him.

"I see that."

"I could meet you there," Ginny said.

Karina didn't respond. She wasn't sure if she trusted herself to be alone with him. But Ginny took her silence as agreement and rushed down the stairs to slip past Damien and out the door. Still Karina said nothing while Damien climbed the stairs to where she was standing.

"I miss you," he whispered.

Karina shook her head. "Why are you here?" she asked.

"I told you, I want to talk to you. I need to explain."

To explain. To explain why he had to let her go, she imagined.

"You can't do this to me, Damien," she said, her voice cracking.

"Please," he pleaded.

She sighed before turning around and heading back up the stairs with him following her. He stood right behind her as she unlocked the door, and the heat of his body brought back so many memories. Memories she didn't need to be thinking about if she was going to protect her heart.

They walked in, and Damien shut the door behind him.

"What is it you wanted to say?" she asked, turning to face him while leaving enough space between them.

He stood there by the door, staring at the ground.

"I rehearsed it so many times in my head the past few days," he said. "And now…."

"This is exactly what I was afraid of," she said, reaching around him for the door.

"Wait," he said, grabbing her arm. "You kept asking why I wanted you in Miami with me, and I wasn't able to give an answer."

"Tell me something I don't know," she said, wrenching her arm from his grip, and he frowned.

"When I came into the coffee shop that morning," he said, "the line was long. And as I looked at the front of it, trying to decide if I should just send Tom in, I saw you. I continued to watch you as the line progressed, laughing and smiling with the customers. It was mesmerizing." He touched her face, and this time she didn't stop him. "Then you turned around and our eyes locked, and it was as if the world stood still. I couldn't understand it."

Karina could still remember that moment when she first saw Damien like it was yesterday. It had literally taken her breath away.

"After I left," he continued. "I couldn't stop thinking about you. I even went back the next morning, but you weren't there."

"I closed that night," she said, and he nodded.

"I grabbed a business card on my way out. Not really sure why, but it made me feel connected to you somehow."

"I saw it," she said. "By your bed."

He nodded again before continuing.

"When I ran into you outside the library, I decided I wasn't going to let you slip through my fingers this time. And even though you declined my invitation to dinner, I knew you had felt something too. You didn't try to pull your hand away when I impulsively grabbed it," he said, moving his hand from her face to her hand, lacing his fingers through hers. "I hoped that meant something, so I came back that night and you explained your situation. Somewhat. I thought if I offered to help and you accepted, then you must be feeling something as well."

Karina remembered how pained Damien had been when she told him in New York that she had been going to change her mind. It all made sense now.

"I had seen your full name on one of the papers you dropped," he explained. "Since you were looking at graduate programs, I knew you must have already been a student, so I started with the same school and immediately found you. And then you agreed to my proposition. But you made yourself sick that first night," he said as his face twisted into something else. "And I was worried about you, and even that emotion surprised me. It occurred to me that you drank so much because you were afraid of me, so I gave you space. It's the only reason I ran off to LA. I could've handled everything from home. I thought maybe I had been wrong about you," he said, shaking his head. "That you hadn't agreed because you wanted to be with me, but because of what I was doing for you. That you were like everyone else. And it was breaking my heart." He sighed before continuing. "But when I came home, you came downstairs. Just being in the same room with you reminded me how much I wanted you. And you no longer seemed afraid of me."

He took her other hand.

"I heard you come to my bedroom door that night," he said. "You turned the handle even. But you didn't come in."

"I was confused," she whispered.

"About what?"

"About you. About what I was starting to feel for you."

"I'm in love with you, Karina," he said. "I think I have been since the moment I laid eyes on you. And it terrifies me. I've never felt this way. I couldn't even recognize it at first. Not until you told me you wanted to go home early. When you told me that…well, it was a pain I never imagined."

Damien lifted both her hands to his lips, and Karina felt her eyes water.

"I was a fool for letting you walk out the door."

"You were an asshole," she laughed, and a tear slid down her cheek.

"I was," he said, wiping the tear away. "I don't deserve you. But that doesn't mean I'll stop trying to prove how much you mean to me. I love you, Karina. Please come home with me. Please go to school in Miami." He took a deep breath. "I don't want to remember what my life was like without you. Let me show you how much I love you. *Amorecito, me cielo.* You are my world."

"Is that what that means?"

He nodded. "Technically it translates to 'my sky,' but same thing." He pressed his forehead to hers. "You are my sky, my sun, my everything. And I'm sorry it took me so long to say it to you."

"Did you just apologize to me?" she asked with a smile.

"I did," he said, smiling back. "I think I owe you some music, don't I?"

She nodded.

"Does that mean you'll come with me?"

"Yes," she said, and Damien pressed his lips to hers as he lifted her off the ground and spun her in a circle.

"I love you," he said, setting her feet back on the floor. "I'll say it a hundred times every day if I have to. Anything to have you at my side."

"I love you too," she said. "And I'll say it back a hundred times if I have to for you to remember it."

Epilogue

KARINA AND GINNY stood in the foyer talking to her parents.

"So are you going to start the job hunt soon?" her mother asked.

"Not just yet," Karina said cryptically.

"Just because your boyfriend's a billionaire doesn't mean you shouldn't use that new fancy degree of yours," Ginny said.

"I'm sure that's not what Karina is implying," her father said before narrowing his eyes at her. "Right?"

She shrugged and was spared having to say anything else by a waiter coming around with a tray of champagne.

"For the toast," he told them.

She looked at him in confusion until Damien walked up, already carrying his own glass.

"May I borrow Karina for a moment?" he asked, and everyone nodded.

"What's going on?" she asked as she let him lead her over to the stairs.

"What kind of host would I be if I didn't congratulate the graduate," he said. They walked up a couple of steps, just enough so that everyone's face was in view.

"Don't embarrass me," she said with a nervous smile.

"I'll try not to," he said, kissing her cheek before turning to the crowd in his home. "May I have everyone's attention?"

All the guests looked in their direction, and Karina could feel herself blushing already.

"I want to thank you all for coming tonight," he said, "to help celebrate Karina's achievement. I've never seen anyone work as hard as she has these past two years. Especially the last couple of months, where as part of her capstone project, she has been helping me establish the Bishop Community Health Center, something I think we're both very proud of," he said, putting an arm around her.

"Despite all the speculation," he continued, "I've yet to name a director for the program. What Karina didn't know until this morning was that I'd been hoping she would fill that role. And I am thrilled to announce that she has accepted."

Everyone clapped, and Karina could see a couple heads nodding as though they knew it. Tom gave her a wink from the crowd. How he managed to keep it from her, she'd never know.

"If I could have your attention just a little bit longer," Damien said, and everyone quieted again. "What Karina doesn't know is that I still have one more important question."

Karina looked out at Tom, who looked just as baffled as her, and then to Damien, who was getting down on one knee, pulling a little blue box from his pocket, and she gasped.

"Karina Watson, will you marry me?"

"Oh my god, Damien," she whispered. "Yes. Yes, yes, yes!"

The guests all cheered as he stood and slipped the diamond ring on her finger.

"Before you," he said quietly enough so that only she could hear, "I thought true love was impossible, a charade. Now I can't imagine spending a day without you. I love you, Karina, with all my heart."

"I love you, Damien, with all of mine."

He pulled her into him, enveloping her in his arms, and in a kiss. The rest of the crowd melted away from her thoughts, and Karina knew she was right where she belonged.

The most important sentiment my father drilled in to me was thank you. No matter what, you always say thank you. So thank you to Tama, Andrea, Liz, and Cattigan for beta-reading this project that I have been beyond excited about since day one. Thank you to my editor Carrie for helping me polish it. Thank you to my husband for his support and for picking up take-out because I couldn't—didn't want to stop working. And a big thank you to my readers for giving me a reason to keep doing this. I know I'd probably be doing it anyway, but thank you for making it feel worthwhile. Your love and support makes my heart swell.

As a kid, I wanted to be a lot of things when I grew up. Strangely enough, being a writer wasn't one of them, no matter how much I was doing it in my spare time. I never did decide what I wanted to do, and for that I am grateful because I might not being doing this now if I were too busy with a "real" job. I've managed to experience a lot in my lifetime, both good and bad, and I love drawing from it all to create my stories. So while the tales you read are completely made up, my heart and soul are still sprinkled among the pages.

If you'd like to know more about me, come find me on social media!

Fb.com/AlexStrongWrites
Twitter and Instagram: @TheAlex_Strong